TWO IN ONE

The man's jaw dropped when he saw Lee Morgan, unable to move in his wonderment over how Morgan had gotten inside. When his mouth finally began to move, Lee shot him through the chest. His arms shot out to his sides and his entire torso flew backward through the window, sending blood, shattered glass, and bits of wood falling through the air.

The other man witnessed his companion's fall and turned quickly to confront their attacker. He hadn't even raised his weapon when Lee put a shot into his head, sending him flying against the wall, his hands clutching the gaping wound between his eyes. The man was oblivious to the fact that the back of his skull no longer existed.

Also in the *Buckskin* Series:

BUCKSKIN #18

REMINGTON RIDGE

KIT DALTON

LEISURE BOOKS NEW YORK CITY

A LEISURE BOOK®

September 2004

Published by

Dorchester Publishing Co., Inc.
200 Madison Avenue
New York, NY 10016

ISBN 0-8439-2509-4

Visit us on the web at www.dorchesterpub.com.

1

There was nothing Lee Morgan liked better than the solitary, quiet feeling of lying under the stars by a big orange fire on a cool autumn night, of being alone except for the sounds of the miles of wilderness around him and the fathomless blackness above him.

Tonight was one of those nights, except that he wasn't quite alone. In a deep sleep and curled beside him lay Lisa Anderson. Though she had known many men in her life as one of New Orleans' abundant prostitutes, at this moment she looked every bit the innocent child. Her dark brown hair was pulled back into a tight ponytail and her thin face, made pale in the moonlight, gave her an angelic appearance.

As beautiful and desirable as she was,

Lee Morgan had to wonder what had possessed him to allow her to talk him into bringing her back to Spade Bit. Though she was one of the feistiest women Lee had ever met, she had been city born and bred. And she had been educated in one of the finest schools the city had to offer. What right had he to take her away from what was a promising future? Though she had suffered a terrible setback at Madam Rosa's boarding house, Lisa would have eventually charmed her way to success and prosperity. But now, almost a thousand miles away from her home, away from every last shred of culture, Lisa looked more at home sharing Lee's bedroll than she ever had in the plush surroundings of one of New Orleans' most notorious brothels.

Lee's eyes widened at the snap of the first twig, and by the time the nearby horses had begun to stir, he was groping for the holster laying by his side. His first thought was that some small animal was prowling around the camp looking for leftovers from their sparse supper. But he wasn't taking any chances. A gun in hand was always a safe tack, especially when sleeping out in the open.

A second snap and the horses screamed almost in unison. Lee glanced to his side and saw that Lisa was still sleeping, oblivious to everything but dreams of the unbridled passion of the afternoon before. A smile still lingered on her lips. Lee eased aside the heavy woolen blanket that sheltered both of them against the night air and inched his way to his feet in a crouch. The horses were prancing nervously and would have bolted had they not been tied. Lee saw nothing else move, even in the light of the full moon. There was simply no place an intruder could hide. The nearest trees were fifty yards away, and at that distance neither he nor the horses would have heard the footsteps. Lee rubbed his eyes against sleep and the smoke from the smoldering remains of the fire that had not long before ceased to blaze.

The only other shelter was the boulder, the mammoth rock by which the two horses were tied to a lone tree. Whoever made the noise must be behind the rock, Lee figured, hidden in the moon's shadow, waiting for just the right moment to make his play. Lee was just about to lay low so as to make himself less of a target, when he saw the tracks near his bedroll, tracks that did not belong to another man.

And then he heard it, the distinct low growl of a mountain lion. Before Lee could stand again, the cougar leaped from the back of the boulder to the top, and then onto the appaloosa's back in a motion as smooth as water flowing down a river. The lion again let out a terrible cry, and Lisa sat straight up in the bedroll, trembling with the terror of the moment. The thick blanket was clutched tightly under her chin. She stared with wide eyes at Lee, unable to speak or scream.

Lee took steady aim at the wildcat and fired off a round. He saw a flash of spark as the slug hit the stone. The big cat sensed the danger but did not run. Lee guessed that the animal must have been starving for it not to run off at the sound of his warning shot. No sooner had Lee fired than the beast left the bleeding, crying horse for this new challenge. Lee barely had time to aim again before the cat was rushing toward him. Just as it leaped, Lee squeezed off another round, cursing himself for not having killed it with the first shot. As soon as the shot sounded, Lee hit the ground. If he missed, the cat would be right on top of him, and no amount of wrestling with it would save him then. He didn't even have his knife on him. And that wasn't the worst of it. Lisa would be defenseless, with no gun and no place to run. Even if she made it to one unhurt horse, their speed would be no match for the cat's.

The animal tumbled onto the ground behind him, and Lee turned just in time to see it get back to its feet, blood oozing from a torn ear, its snarling face anxious for Lee's flesh. The cat was even madder than before and Lee knew that he would not have another chance. The cat was preparing to pounce and Lee had dropped his gun in his fall. It was quiet for a moment as the two creatures stared at one another, Lee hoping desperately that he could sidestep the attack, the cat confident in its victory. It was then that Lee heard the shot, and the big cat roared and fell, writhing onto its side. Within seconds it was dead, as peaceful as Lee would have been had the cat not awakened him.

When Lee looked at Lisa, she was still holding the smoking .44 at arm's length before her. "Where'd you find the gun?" Lee asked, amazed that they were both not dead. Lisa did not answer or move, her eyes never leaving the fallen animal.

Lee walked back to the bedroll and eased the gun from the girl's shaking hand. Her eyes were still filled with terror, and Lee took her trembling body in his powerful arms, comforting her as if she were a wounded animal.

"Thank you," he said and planted a tender kiss on her forehead. She spread her arms around his naked chest and pulled him close. She shivered and Lee pulled the heavy blanket around her shoulders against her goose bumps. As the chill went through her, Lee could feel her nipples harden against his chest. Desire quickly overcame him as he tried to urge Lisa back onto the bedroll. Instead, Lisa took him in a passionate embrace. Releasing his grip, he nuzzled her neck and kissed the way down to her breasts. They were taut and white and small enough that Lee had no trouble taking the entire breast in his mouth. He slowly rolled his tongue over the nipple, sucking it, nipping it with his teeth, making it stand out even farther.

Lisa moaned as the desire she felt whenever he was near overwhelmed her once again. Despite her chill, Lisa let the coarse blanket fall from her shoulders and down her back. Her milky skin shone in the moonlight as Lee ran his hands over her lithe body, warming her with his own heat and teasing her neck and ear with his tongue. Lisa finally gave in to Lee's gentle pushes and lay on her back on the bedroll. She stretched her neck full length as Lee continued with his urgent kisses. She tore at Lee's flannel shirt until he stopped to throw it off. While Lee was still sitting, Lisa made her move for his belt buckle, not for a moment considering how vulnerable she and Lee would be should they be approached by another wild animal. There was just one wild animal Lisa had on her mind at the moment, and that was Lee Morgan.

Lisa hurriedly unfastened his belt and undid his trouser buttons with one swift tug. She pulled the pants and long johns over his hips until she was staring at the object of her desire—the magnificent organ that hung between his corded legs, the same organ that had again and again given her so much pleasure. Now she desired him in earnest. While Lee finished removing his jeans, Lisa lay back again, watching the swelling begin between Lee's legs. She unhooked the crudely fashioned buckskin skirt they had picked up for her along the road back to Spade Bit. Resting on her shoulders and lifting her buttocks high into the air, she slid the skirt over her hips and lay it neatly beside the bedroll. Lee had seated himself before her to watch the show of Lisa contorting her body to remove the last of her clothing. Lisa noticed that his cock was standing almost full length before him and, as if to coax it to the bursting point, she swung one of her legs over Lee's head and wrapped them both around his waist. The view of Lisa's slender legs holding his body and the sight of the mysterious dark patch joining them was almost too much for Lee to take. Lisa stared down her body at Lee's newly excited member. Even in the dim moonlight she could see that his organ had changed from a baby pink to a swollen purpling rod fit for a queen. And that's just what she intended to be as long as Lee would have her. And it was her one desire that that would be for as long as they lived.

With her legs still around Lee, Lisa sat up and took his cock in her fingers, sliding the loose skin back and forth until a bead of semen appeared at the tip. She dipped her finger into the drop and coated the head of his organ with a slippery film, making it ready to enter her. Lisa was already as wet as she had been since the first time they had made love three months before. The hair around her opening was drenched with her womanly juices.

Lee teased her with his fingers, gently probing her swollen opening and massaging the little bulb hidden within her folds of flesh. Then he stopped his teasing and slid one calloused finger easily inside. Lisa stiffened and fell back onto the bedroll, writhing in her passion as Lee worked one finger, then another, deep within her. With his other hand, Lee spread Lisa's legs and kneaded the inside of her thighs, feeling the muscles grow tigher with his every stroke. With one swift movement, Lee stretched his body over her and replaced his fingers with his throbbing member, feeling the heat generating in her body and the tender stroke of her fingers across his back.

From her gasps and the contortions of her body, Lee knew that it wouldn't take much to send Lisa into the throes of an orgasm. Sliding his arms under her legs, Lee lifted her thighs high into the air. Lisa lifted her ass and rode Lee's every move, sliding in closer with each thrust of his hips until the full length of him was inside her. When she reached the hilt, her moans and gasps were almost as loud as the mountain lion's screams had been.

Her orgasm was intense, drawing every ounce of strength from her soul. As frightening as her ordeal had been, all danger was forgotten as wave after wave of pleasure swept through her. All that was left was the cool autumn night and the heat of Lee Morgan's body comforting her.

Though Lisa's body was now sated and limp, Lee did not cease his savage thrusts. He was too far gone to stop for rest. There was nothing left but Lisa's smooth body and the desire to let his tightening balls release their load deep into Lisa's quivering hole. As she returned to her senses, Lisa began to respond to his desperate thrusts with small little thrusts of her own. Lee lifted his weight from her body by raising up on his elbows, and Lisa saw this as a chance to excite him even further. She ran her fingers through the thick blond hair on his chest and pinched his nipples as he had done to her. Finally, she tightened her cunt around his cock and countered Lee's every move. Lisa's attentions did not go unnoticed. Lee's load was on the verge of bursting with all the force of a fire hose. One of Lisa's hands made its way between his legs and around the sac which held his balls. All it took was a gentle squeeze and Lee hollered in ecstasy. If another wildcat had jumped on his back at that very moment, it could not have torn him away. Burst after burst of hot semen shot deep into Lisa's hole, so much that they both thought that it might overflow. Even after he came, Lee kept pumping her, savoring every second of the delicious union.

When at last he was limp again, Lee pulled out of her, causing Lisa to give a little gasp as the tip came free. Both were utterly spent and exhausted. The days of hard travel and the hours of passionate lovemaking finally caught up with them and neither said a word as they nestled in each other's arms and fell into a dreamless sleep.

High above, in the clear Idaho sky, two vultures sailed and soared on the air currents produced by the mountain passes of the Rockies. Below, Lee Morgan could almost feel their ravenous stares as they glided directly overhead. Stretched out on a lush bed of grass, Lee was wondering what had brought them out so early when he remembered the carnage of the night before. It was careless of him not to dispose of the mountain lion's carcass, and even more careless of him not to have tended to the horse's wounds. Though they were almost home and the walk would not be a great ordeal, horseflesh was more valuable than gold in Lee Morgan's mind, and if the wounded animal were severely hurt it, would be his own damn fault.

By the time he remembered the vultures, the great birds had circled down a hundred feet or so, and Lee was reminded of the times when he was a kid. He would sometimes sit still for hours in some forgotten corner of Spade Bit and watch a mountain hawk circle above with a watchful eye, and stare in awe as it swooped into dense brush and emerged with a squirming mouse held fast in its needlelike talons.

As the vultures dropped still lower, Lee roused himself and shook Lisa awake. Her groggy eyes peeled themselves open and then quickly shut again against the brilliance of the rising sun. Lisa pulled the wool blanket over her head and feigned sleep while Lee got the fire going again.

While the last of the coffee perked over the open flame, Lee grabbed one of the saddle bags and walked over to inspect the two grazing horses. From the fire, the appaloosa did not seem to be harmed, but as Lee approached, he could see several scabbing cuts on the animal's bare back. Though minor, Lee realized that he and Lisa would be walking home after all. A saddle and rider on the horse's back would only irritate the wounds and be painful for the animal. The horse shied away when Lee approached but its fright eased when it recognized the man. Lee ran his hands over the animal's smooth skin, then reached into the saddle bag for his jar of salve. The horse jumped at the renewed burning as Lee spread the salve over the cuts, but calmed again when Lee offered a sugar cube as a reward for being so tolerant. The horse gratefully crushed it with his powerful molars and went back to grazing on the sparse grass by the boulder.

As Lee moved both horses to the other side where the grass was more plentiful, he couldn't help but wonder how the rock got there in the first place. The nearest precipice was several hundred yards away, so it could not have fallen. And it certainly did not form there naturally. But he did not dwell on this. Maybe it had been rolled there many years ago to serve as some sort of Indian shrine. Though he couldn't figure it, neither did he care. There was not much on Lee Morgan's mind except getting safely back to Spade Bit and seeing how his men had fared in his absence.

Back at the camp, the smell of the fresh coffee had roused Lisa from her blissful slumber. Fully dressed now, she was sitting by the fire vainly trying to put together a quick breakfast of oatmeal and jerky. Lee had suffered several of Lisa's breakfasts and wasn't looking forward to spending the rest of the day trying to clear his throat of lumpy mush and picking burned coffee grounds from between his teeth.

"Why don't you start packing up the camp while I do the honors this morning?" Lee said, smiling while gently taking the sack of oats from Lisa's hands. "It ain't right for a lady, especially my lady, to cook on the trail. There'll be plenty of time and opportunity for cooking once we get back to the ranch. There ain't one of my boys 'cept Charlie can cook worth a damn. They'll be mightly pleased to find that there'll be a woman in the kitchen again."

Lisa gave him a queer look and sheepish smile and guessed that Lee was having a bit of fun at her expense. But she wasn't about to argue with the man who had rescued her from a miserable life of prostitution in New Orleans. After brushing off her skirt, she turned to pack up the bed roll, but not before getting in a little jab of her own. "Hope that oatmeal isn't as runny as your mouth, Mr. Morgan," she said, looking over her shoulders. Lee chuckled and threw a handful into the pot of boiling water.

"Just have to know how to measure it, ma'am," he said, mocking her tone. Then, on a more serious note, he added, "We're gonna have to eat quick this morning. I want to get back on the trail as soon as we get this place cleaned up."

"You're missing the ranch pretty bad, aren't you?" Lisa asked as she tied up the bedroll with a piece of rope.

"Missing home ain't got nothing to do with it. You looked up in the sky lately?" Lee began stirring the oatmeal as vigorously as if he were beating a cake batter.

Lisa tilted her head skyward to see what the hell he was talking about. She knew good and well there wasn't a cloud in the sky. Hadn't been for days. A gasp caught in her throat when Lisa saw the giant raptors circling above, and though Lee's back was turned, he knew she was too startled to speak.

"W-what are they?" Lisa stammered, and she scampered over to where Lee was adding more water to the already runny oatmeal. Lee saw the fear in her eyes and wished he hadn't alarmed her.

"Vultures," he said quietly. "They're after that cat you shot last night. Been up there since first light."

Lisa squeezed his arm and pulled herself even closer. "Will they attack us?" she asked.

Lee looked at her as if she were crazy, but then remembered that Lisa was city born and bred. She had no knowledge of the outdoor life at all. Every vista and every creature was new to her. Lee wondered how she would ever fit in once back on the ranch. As naive as she was, Lee had made it clear before they left New Orleans that she would have to pull her own weight once in Idaho. Women in the west were different than those back east. They worked hard, they wore practical clothes, and most important, they were a very independent lot. It wasn't without a good bit of arguing that Lee had agreed to let her return with him. He'd used every reason he could think of to convince her to stay in the east, but in the end he'd even given in to letting her stay at the ranch until she got settled. But he had vowed that if by the end of the winter she were not established on her own, she would be on a train bound for New Orleans. Surely Madam Rosa would put her up again until she found a suitable husband. Idaho might be a paradise for the strong hearted, but for a woman of weak constitution, he

21

was convinced it would be sheer hell.

"Not unless we drop dead right here," Lee was saying. "They might look fierce, but they won't light until a while after we're gone. They like to eat in private. And don't you worry none about one of 'em swooping down on you. They're more afraid of you than you are of them. They only eat dead bodies. Scavengers is what they are."

"Maybe we should bury the cat," Lisa said sheepishly.

"What the hell for? Vultures have to eat breakfast too."

"It just seems so . . . so barbaric."

"Ha!" Lee laughed. "Barbaric! If you came out here to find manners, we might just as well turn around right now. If you think they're barbaric, wait till you meet some of the folks back in Grover. Most of them are so ornery they'd pick your pocket if you didn't keep your hands in them." Lee dipped the ladle into the steaming oatmeal broth and sloshed a serving for each of them into the bowls he had set aside. Lisa pulled herself free from Lee's side and poured them both a cup of the overdone coffee.

"Lee, are you mad at me?"

Lee looked into her eyes. "Now, what the hell gave you that idea?" But Lee knew exactly what had given her the idea. He had been short with her, and had come close to making fun of her lack of experience in matters that were second nature to him. And if there was one thing a woman hated more than anything else, that was to be made fun of by a man.

"You just seem so . . . cold this morning. Are you starting to feel sorry that you brought me along? I'll understand if you are. I know I practically begged you to bring me back with you. If you're tired of me already, I'll take the first train back."

"Now you get that idea out of your head right this minute. If I hadn't wanted you to come, you wouldn't be here now. Nothing on earth would have made me bring you if I hadn't wanted to." Lee brushed her black hair back and kissed her hard on the lips. "Now, there'll be no more talk about you taking any trains out of here. Hell, you haven't even given it a chance yet. And don't let my teasing get to you. You know I don't mean nothing by it. 'Sides, that's just a taste of what you're apt to get once we get back to the ranch." Lee picked up his spoon again and slurped down another mouthful of the watery oatmeal. "Finish up your coffee. We've still got a few hours of riding ahead of us, and with that horse hurt, most of it will have to be on foot."

Lisa smiled at him, embarrassed that she had acted like such a baby in his presence. Of course Lee was right. If she were going to make it in this rugged country, she was going to have to be stronger. Still, she couldn't help but cast nervous glances toward the sky whenever Lee was not looking.

It took less than twenty minutes to finish eating and packing. Lisa couldn't get ready fast enough. Their belongings were saddled to the one good horse, while the other was tethered to the lead horse's saddle. As Lee was cinching up the last of the packs Lisa screamed and grabbed Lee around the waist. "What is it?" Lee hollered.

Lisa covered her mouth with one hand and pointed toward the camp with the other. Lee was about to chastise her for making another of her silly outbursts when he happened to see what she was pointing at. There, not thirty paces away, the first of the vultures had lit and was slowly stalking the remains of the dead mountain lion.

Lee stood with his hands on his hips and stared bemused. "I'll be damned," he said. "Never known one of those buzzards to drop down when folks were around. Damn things must be starving to death."

"It would be just fine with me if they did," Lisa said, pulling at Lee's arm. "May we get out of here now? Call me what you like, Lee, but I don't think I can bear to watch them tear that animal apart. It's bad enough that I had to kill it in the first place."

"What!" Lee exclaimed in mock astonishment. "Now you're feeling sorry for the creature that nearly tore me to ribbons last night. Be thankful that you did kill it, darlin'. Otherwise those buzzards might be getting their fill of us this morning."

"Goodness! Lee can we please get out of here now? I don't think I can stand another minute of this."

Lee chuckled and finished cinching up the bags. Then the two of them began quickly walking north once again, Lisa looking over her shoulder every few moments to make sure none of the birds had decided that the cat didn't hit the spot.

In September the days were much shorter than they had been on that June day that Lee Morgan had decided to pack up his things for Timothy O'Sullivan's disastrous Panama expedition. His friend Sam had been right. Lee had had his fill of wild times. It was not a time to be going on crazy adventures like the one he was now returning from. Luckily he was returning with his skin intact. Though his reflexes hadn't diminished a whit, he had nearly lost his life on several occasions during his encounters with some of the fiercest Indians south of the border. Now, within a few miles of home, he was relieved to be coming back to what he had so desperately tried to escape: the drudgery of life as owner of the Spade Bit Ranch. It seemed to him odd, but the thought of managing the books, of issuing instructions, of paying tedious visits to Grover's business elite, was suddenly a welcome image. If he never saw another Indian or outlaw again, it would be too soon. If he never again tasted the life of an adventurer that would be just fine with him. Once back on Spade Bit, he would devote the rest of his life to managing the ranch. He had stuck his neck out for someone else for the last time. Perhaps he'd even get married again.

The thought of marriage brought home again the dilemma he had been wrestling with since he had agreed to bring Lisa back to Spade Bit with him; What to do about his courtship with Suzanne Clemons. Surely the poor girl must be half out of her mind with worry for him by now. He'd been gone over three months and had left without so much as saying goodbye to her. Half the town was aware that he had been sweet on her, and there wasn't a Friday night that went by that the two of them couldn't be seen walking down Main Street in their Sunday best, arm and arm and oblivious to everything and everyone around them. He knew that most had expected him to propose before he unexpectedly took off on O'Sullivan's ill-fated adventure. Now he was returning with a beautiful young woman in tow. There were bound to be rumors and enough malicious gossip to make both him and Suzanne the talk of the town once again.

He had to plan carefully if he were to live down this mistake. He was immensely attracted to Lisa, but he also had an obligation to Suzanne. If it came down to choosing between the two, he would have to choose Suzanne, so strong was his feeling for her—that is, if she would still have him. Once back at Spade Bit, Lisa would have to make her own way. Lee had made it clear that he would not marry her, no matter how much she begged. And if Lee could help it, his relationship with Lisa would never be brought to Suzanne's attention. In all likelihood, Lisa would not be able to stand up to the hardships of the Western life and would soon be on a train returning to Madam Rosa's in New Orleans. After all, the men in Grover did not come from the same cultured breeding as Lisa, and there would be few potential husbands even in Boise.

Lee quickened his gait and had to admire the fact that Lisa was not complaining about keeping up with him. She matched his progress step for step without comment, even taking her turn leading the horses. At least she's trying, Lee thought. That's more than most women of her background would do. Any other woman would have me carrying her on my back by now.

The camp was miles behind them now and the sun was as high as it could get on a September day. The terrain was rocky one moment and a flat expanse of grass the next, as they skirted foothills and slowly made their way northward. Lee figured it would be midafternoon before Spade Bit came into view, and then another hour before they crossed the range of Lee's land and reached the sturdy house Lee and his men had constructed after it had been burned by the Jack Mormons over a year before. He hoped there had been no more trouble with them while he was away. Lee was sure the ranch was in good hands. Luke was an able foreman, despite his drinking problem. And Sam was as reliable a man as he would ever find. In all likelihood, Spade Bit would be exactly as he had left it. The entire operation running with the precision of a fine Swiss timepiece.

Lisa finally broke down and said she wanted to rest and eat. After all, they had been walking for hours and the going was a far cry from a Sunday stroll. Lee couldn't agree with her more. His feet were aching so bad that nothing else had been on his mind for the last couple of miles. All he wanted to do was pull off his boots and dunk his swollen feet into a soapy tub of steaming water.

They sat in the shade of an immense fir tree that had probably been standing for a century before Lee Morgan had been born. The afternoon was far from cool, but the warmth from the sun was nothing compared to the oppressive heat Lee had faced in Panama and at the mouth of the Mississippi. Lee broke out what was left of the biscuits they had picked up the day before and then surprised Lisa with a little crock of jam he had bought to surprise her. After a feast of this, a taste of jerky, and a few swigs of the stale water from the canteens, the two lay back for a rest before hitting the trail again.

"Well, kid, we've damn near made it," Lee said, as he picked his teeth with a bit of grass he had pulled for that purpose. He glanced over to see Lisa looking at the magnificent cloud formations above—or was she looking out for vultures? "There was a time when I never wanted to see that old ranch again. Now here I am champing at the bit to get back to it. Crazy, ain't it?"

Lisa turned her distant stare directly into Lee's eyes. "If your ranch is anything like the country I've seen so far, I'd say your daddy was about the sanest man that ever lived. There's nothing in New Orleans to compare to this. I've never seen so much green in all my life."

"You think I'd bring you back here if it weren't anything close to the Garden of Eden? It took a good chunk out of my Alaska strike to buy this place back. But I figger it's worth it. It was getting to be about time I settled down and there ain't no place to do it than where my daddy raised me. I once thought settling down was about the worst thing in the world a man could do, but right now it feels just right."

The rest of the trip was relatively easy going. The hills sloped gently and the trail was well marked. At the top of a rise around three in the afternoon, Lee suddenly stopped and pointed through the thinning trees to a wisp of smoke attached to a building in the distance. "Spade Bit," he said.

"It's positively beautiful!" Lisa exclaimed. "Even more so than you said."

Suddenly Lee wasn't interested in the sight of home. What had caught his eye was the three riders patrolling the outlying border of his ranch at the bottom of the hill, three riders he did not recognize. Maybe they were just passing through, but then again, maybe they were rustlers scouting out the country. Whoever they were, Lee was not about to take any chances by giving away his presence. "Get down!" he snapped, taking Lisa by surprise.

"What? What are you talking about?" Lisa said as she was forced to the ground by Lee's heavy hand.

"I said get down, and stay down," Lee said with violence in his voice. "Don't you see those men down there?"

"Of course I see them! Aren't they your own men?"

"I don't know whose men they are, but they're sure not mine. Look how heavily armed they are. My boys would never be so loaded down with weapons 'less there was something wrong. And it's my guess that those men down there are definitely something wrong." Lee pulled out his Colt and made sure he had plenty of rounds on him. "Now, look, I want you to stay down here and mind the horses. Keep low and don't move from this spot until I get back. I'm going down there to see what this is all about. It's probably nothing, but I want to be sure before we go riding into something we don't know anything about."

"You think they might be dangerous?" Lisa looked worried now, even more so than when she first spotted the vultures.

"Anything's possible, but I'd rather be safe than sorry. I guess I'll know as soon

as I show my face. If they mean us any harm, at least you'll be out of the way."
Lee backed the horses a way down the side of the hill where they had just come from and tied the lead animal to a low tree branch, hoping that he and Lisa wouldn't have to make a hasty retreat. After checking to make sure both of his Colts were fully loaded, Lee gestured again for Lisa to keep her head down and then strode down the side of the hill toward the riders. As he stepped lower, the underbrush became thicker and he was able to approach without being seen. When he was within earshot, Lee dropped into a crouch and strained to hear the bits and pieces of agitated conversation.

"What the hell we gotta spend the day snooping around the border of Morgan's land for anyway?" came the first voice. "Ain't there enough to do back on the ranch? Paxton said he wanted the place fixed up from top to bottom before that banker fellow took ownership."

Then a second voice: "Aw, quit your griping. You oughta be grateful that we're getting to go out riding instead of brushing down them goddamn horses. 'Sides, it's only for a few more days. Morgan aint' shown up yet. Everyone's given him up for dead. An' just as soon as the deed is transfered back to the bank, we get our cut, Paxton gets his share, and everyone is happy."

So that was their game! Lee couldn't believe his ears. Paxton! Billy Paxton! The very thought of the name set the hairs on the back of Lee's neck on end. So he was back . . . the son-of-a-bitch who had had his wife shot down in cold blood was back for another try at his ranch.

But he wondered where the third man had gone. He had spied three riders from the ridge above them. One of them had disappeared and might be sneaking up on him at that very moment for all he knew. Lee crouched lower, anticipating an attack and looking for an opportunity to make a move himself.

The shot in the distance resounded clearly, but Lee could not tell from which direction it came. The two riders near him at once looked startled and worried. Since these men were hirelings of Paxton's and not poachers after all, Lee figured that he had been spotted and the shot had been a warning from the missing rider to the two on horseback. Without waiting to find out the significance, Lee rose from the brush and leveled his Colt at the man he assumed was the leader of the three.

"You down there," Lee yelled. "Both of you toss down those sidearms and walk away from those horses." The two men looked at each other and then back at Lee, both with a malicious gleam in their eyes. Lee sensed that neither man knew who he was, nor did they have any intention of doing as he had commanded.

"Now!" he yelled again, gesturing with the barrel of his revolver. "Or you're both dead men."

Either the two men did not believe that one man could take on the pair of them from that distance armed with only a handgun, or they were all too willing to risk their lives for the man who had hired them, but they both unfastened the scabbards holding the rifles at the sides of their horses. Lee wasn't left with much choice. The lead man was the obvious target. Lee dropped to one knee, aimed, and pulled off a shot that caught the lead rider square in the throat. Suddenly blood was everywhere. The shot nearly severed the man's head as it exploded into his neck. His head shot back and blood spurted out onto his shirt and the fine horse he rode—one of Lee's best stallions. Then the man's head tumbled forward again and Lee saw the man's eyes staring wide as if it were the most natural thing in the world to do at the moment. With his hand still clutched to the rifle butt and one foot trapped in the stirrup, the horse began running, with the rider still attached, back toward home.

The second rider did not even have time to catch what was happening. His spooked animal reared up on its hind legs at the sound of the first shot and pawed the air as if it were trying to break out of a cage. Lee knew the animal well enough to sense that once the horse regained its footing, it would bolt wildly after the first horse, oblivious to any shooting or its rider's commands. Lee couldn't afford to let the horseman escape, even in this manner. If he got back to Spade Bit in one piece, he would tell Paxton and anyone else involved in the fight for his ranch exactly what had happened. If that happened, Paxton would have his men scouring the countryside night and day for Morgan, with orders to shoot him on sight.

So Lee aimed again, hoping to wing the man and get the information he needed to keep whatever plan Paxton had devised from working. He would decide later what to do with the man.

He lined up his shot just as the horse was coming down. He would only have time for one shot and he hoped like hell it would be better than the one he had gotten off against the wildcat the night before. As the horse hit the ground, he pulled the trigger and felt the gun buck in his hand. He knew he had shot true. The man on the horse screamed and clutched at the gaping hole in his chest as the force of the impact threw him off the back of the horse. He landed on his seat sitting up on the dirt, and as he looked at the wound, his eyes rolled slowly back into his head and he fell the rest of the way to the ground.

Lee's aim was not as true as he thought. He didn't even need to check to know that the man was dead. Lee kicked the underbrush away and emerged from the trees with his Colt still at the ready. The third rider might still be lurking about, waiting for him to come into the clearing to get a clean shot at the man who had murdered his compatriots. But Lee's concern was put at ease when he saw the cloud of dust moving rapidly away from him in the distance. Evidently, the man had seen what was happening and chose not to stick around to suffer the same fate.

Lee smiled ruefully to himself, pleased that he still had an edge on even the slickest of gunmen. It wasn't every man who could dispatch three gunmen with two shots. But his smile was quickly replaced with a scowl. Paxton had somehow managed to take his ranch, and it was going to take every bit of his cunning to get it back.

Strangely, the second rider's horse had not bolted as he had expected. Instead, it was grazing peacefully on the autumn-dried grass some yards away. Lee's sharp whistle brought its ears to erection as it recognized its long-vanished master, the same man who had broken it two years before. The horse pranced over to Lee, nosing his shoulder to make sure it was really him. Lee took the horse's reins and gave it a quick inspection. Whatever Paxton might be, at least he was taking good care of Lee's horses.

It suddenly dawned on Lee that he had forgotten all about Lisa waiting on the hill above him. She had surely heard the shots and was probably out of her mind with worry over her benefactor. Lee led the horse back through the brush and trees and began to climb the steep rise to the top of the hill. As he climbed, he glanced over his shoulder several times to make sure that the third rider had not changed his mind and returned to follow him. Lee knew that once the man reached the ranch house, it was only a matter of time before a small army of Paxton's men would be swarming toward the site of the shooting. He and Lisa would have to waste no time making plans to hide out until Lee could get to town to find out just what was going on with his ranch. If Paxton was truly involved in some sort of claim on the place, the bank was equally in on the deal.

At the top of the rise, Lee saw Lisa still laying where he had left her. At second glance he saw that the horses had been untied and wondered what had prompted Lisa to release them. Though the horses had preferred getting their fill on the thick dry grass to running off, Lee was irritated that Lisa had disobeyed him and untied their reins. Had she planned to leave him there?

"Lisa," he called. "How'd the horses get untied? You plannin' on goin' somewhere?"

When there was no answer, Lee refocused his attention on the woman lying on the ground. It suddenly dawned on him that she had not jumped up to greet him. She seemed to be gazing passively toward where the shooting had occured. "Lisa," he called again. "What are you looking at? Is there something happening down there?"

There was no answer. Could she have fallen asleep? he thought. Surely with all the excitement, that could not be possible. Lee quickly walked to her, hoping against hope that nothing had happened to her. But something had happened to her. Lisa had been very dead for at least five minutes, for as long as it had taken the third rider to shoot away the back of her head, untie the horses, and make his escape down the other side of the rise. She probably never knew what hit her. The rider must have crept up behind her and sent her to her maker before he could even yell for help. Lee sat beside her and rolled Lisa onto her side. Her face was expressionless, almost peaceful.

Lee felt his eyes well up with tears, but quickly brushed them aside and went to the horses to get his shovel.

Lee Morgan had a lot of work ahead of him.

2

"What the hell happened?" Billy Paxton was screaming at the young man who had just ridden up with the two horses and the dead man draped over the saddle of the one he was not riding. The man nervously hopped off the side of his mount and handed the reins to a smiling Luke Bransen, who was standing next to Paxton. Bransen took the reins as the man approached Paxton with his head bowed low.

"Hell if I know,"the man was saying. "Me, Billy, and Ray was down at the south end of the spread. There was a glint of something or other up on top of the rise so I went up to check it out. Weren't nothin' there but some girl and a couple of horses. She was laying down and it looked like she was spying on the boys down below. I just made sure she didn't get the chance to do no more peeping where she wasn't supposed to. Then there was some yellin' and a shot down below. I didn't know what the hell was going on. I just got out of there as quick as I could get. Back down the hill I seen Ray's horse trottin' across the meadow with Ray hangin' from the stirrup. There was another shot and I was sure Billy had caught it. I had no way of knowing how many men they were up against. Ray and Billy was good shots. They could take care of themselves in a fix. If someone had killed them, I didn't want nothin' to do with him. I ain't no coward, but I'm smart enough to know when I'm outgunned."

"What you are is a fool," Paxton chided, and slapped the man across the face. "You hear two shots and you run like the cavalry is after you. Where's your guts, man?"

The man stammered and then bowed his head once again in shame for not having pleased the man who paid his generous wages.

"You said there were two horses on the ridge with the woman," Paxton continued, "where was the other rider?"

"Hell if I know," the man answered. "I only know what I saw. He probably went down the ridge to see what was going on and ran into Ray and Billy. If it was just one of them, he was a damn good shot. Ray's got a shot clean through his neck, and that weren't done with no rifle, neither. He's sharp with a sidearm, whoever he is."

Out of the corner of his eye, Paxton saw Luke Bransen's smile get just a little bit wider. "What the hell are you grinnin' at, you goddamn jackal?" Paxton snapped at him.

Bransen immediately put on his usual poker face. "Nothin'," he mumbled, and handed Jim Johnson's ride over to the man on his left. With his hands now empty, he strode over to the horse Ray had been draped across and untied the rope around the man's belt. His form slid limply from the saddle and into the dust, and the flies that had collected on his gaping neck scattered everywhere. Jim had tried to close the wound with his handkerchief, but the blood-soaked rag had come undone and was now hanging from the man's throat by dried blood alone. Bransen thought he was going to be sick, but he knew he was going to have to take care of the body or else risk the wrath of his new keeper. Indicating for two men to get shovels and follow him to the graveyard where Lee's wife was buried, he bent and hoisted the corpse to his shoulders, and carried it quietly out of sight.

"You think it might have been Morgan out there?" Jim Johnson hesitantly asked, his eyes following Bransen and the dead man until they had passed around the corner of the ranch house.

"It don't matter what I think," Paxton said slowly, as if even the mention of Lee Morgan's name might send him into a fit of rage. "As far as you and everyone else is concerned, Morgan is dead. If he ain't, then he will be as soon as he shows his face around here. Now, if you think you're man enough to go back out to that ridge, get a half dozen men and ride back out there. Bring me the girl, the horses, and anything else you can find. And don't bother bringing that coward Billy into my sight. Just bury him where he lays. He ain't fit to have a proper burial." Paxton tore the hat off his head and clomped back indoors, a furious scowl on his face and a terrible look in his eye. Jim nodded at the command but Paxton never saw him. He was too busy trying to figure out just what he was going to do now that Morgan had returned.

Inside the house Paxton sat at the dining table pouring whiskey for the two men on either side of him. They were an unlikely trio, all uneasy with the alliance they had formed and all wary of the other mens' motivations. The man to Paxton's right had initiated the entire scheme. As the town's most powerful leading citizen, the banker Jesse Callaway was still determined to claim Spade Bit as his own and divide the land among the highest-bidding farmers. The fertile land would bring a pretty penny and make Callaway an even richer man than he already was. The man on Paxton's left was slight of build and had a thin, sallow face that bespoke his timid nature. As the town's deputy sheriff, he had built a reputation of looking the other way when gunplay was threatened, but had managed to retain his position only because there was no one else in town who would take it. Callaway had unofficially retained the man as a personal bodyguard. Not that he needed one, but Callaway felt comfortable with giving the impression of power wherever he went. Slight as he was, Chook provided the man with at least the appearance of protection.

Since their last meeting, Paxton had met with a bit of success in his adventures. Selling his services as a regulator had destroyed many lives, but made Paxton a rich man over the past year. He didn't need the money Callaway was offering for his assistance, but he still had a bone to pick with Morgan and would have done anything to see the man dragged through the mud.

"So," he said as he tossed back the first shot of aged whiskey, "it would seem that

Mr. Morgan has returned to regain his land." Callaway's eyes widened at the thought of facing the man who had come close to killing him for attempting to take over his ranch once before. Now, he was within days of taking possession of the ranch once again. If only it wasn't true, if only Morgan had not really returned, it would be his—all his.

"Are you sure?" he asked Paxton. "Couldn't it have been someone else. There's plenty of people in Grover wondering what's going on out here . . ."

"But how many are able to singlehandedly take out two of my men without picking them off from a distance with a long range?" Paxton snapped back. He had convinced himself that Morgan had indeed returned and would certainly pose a formidable threat if allowed to show his face in town.

But who had the girl been? A friend of Morgan's, perhaps? A spy enlisted by him to keep an eye on the ranch? They would soon find out. Johnson would be back in a couple of hours with the woman's body. Surely Morgan was not foolish enough to take the time to bury her. Maybe Deputy Chook or the banker would know her identity. If she was from the town, they would know for certain that Morgan had been there. But why had no one else seen him? Morgan was a striking man and not

45

exactly a master of disguise. If anyone had seen him, it would surely have been reported.

"What do you think we ought to do?" Chook asked no one in particular. "We're already too far into this thing to back down. Half the town knows something funny's goin' on down here, and with Morgan back, all he's got to do is show his face and this whole scheme is going to be open for inspection. The whole lot of us is gonna end up behind bars. You know that, Paxton. We've already locked up Sam Lawton for no reason. Lots of folks in town's been talking about that. I ain't got the right to hold him without just cause. If the law up in Boise finds out about that they'll have my badge."

"I'll have a lot more than your badge if you don't keep him and his big mouth where folks can't hear him. Just you remember. We ain't got a thing to worry about unless Morgan shows his face and gets folks riled up. If he's got a lick of sense, he'll sneak around in town and get the word on what's going on here without showing his face to too many people. I'd be willing to bet that he's going to try to win back his ranch without making a scene. He's got a personal score to settle with me, and if I know him at all, he'll make sure I'm dead before he sees me put behind bars. He knows that if he raises too much fuss, I'll vanish before he ever gets a shot at me. Morgan's smart enough to know that the law around here ain't going to help him. If he wants his goddam ranch back, let him come here and fight for it!''

Callaway looked somewhat relieved. "It'll be him against a dozen of the best guns money can buy." Callaway sighed.

At that moment, if Lee Morgan could have kicked himself, he would have. Lisa's body was in the shallow grave he had dug for her, and now all he had left to do was fill in the hole with dirt. He was nearly in tears as he tossed the first spade full of dirt onto her lifeless form. It would seem that Spade Bit was aptly named. The spade was proving to be the most useful tool he had on the ranch. How many graves had been dug for his friends since his return two years before! He had come back to lead a quiet life as a gentleman rancher, but even when he stayed in one place death followed him like a shadow in autumn. Maybe he'd been wrong about trying to settle down. For a man like himself there was no life without looking to make sure no one was following every few moments. Once a gunman, always a gunman, he thought. There might be more and more people moving out west, but it sure as hell didn't get any safer. Not as long as men like Paxton were allowed to do as they pleased. And men like John Chook let them.

Maybe the law wouldn't do anything to keep Spade Bit from being sold off. But Lee wasn't about to give up without a fight. He never had and never would. He wasn't about to let some tough like Paxton get the best of him. He'd sooner burn the whole ranch than see it fall into Callaway's hands.

Callaway! He was the son-of-a-bitch behind the whole thing. His feud with Paxton was one thing, but knowing that Callaway was involved was quite another. How wrong he had been about the man he had so easily forgiven for trying to take his farm before. He had not even been gone all season and already the man had forgotten every promise he had made, every threat Lee had vowed should he ever try to take Spade Bit from him again.

This time it would be different. There was another girl's death to be avenged. He would show no mercy! Spade Bit would be his again. And no goddamn banker or dandy gunman was going to stand in his way.

Lee slammed the shovel down and packed the rest of the earth above the innocent girl who had lost her life because of his stupidity. It was his own damn fault that he had gone off and left the girl unguarded and unable to defend herself. Lee had vowed to avenge her death, but he hadn't the slighest idea how he was going to do it.

By now, he thought, Paxton should have found out about what had happened back at the ridge. Lee had been smart enough to take the horses and the girl away from the area Paxton's men would be searching. Though Paxton may have suspected that Lee was back, without any evidence, he would have no way of knowing for sure, and Lee would be free to move about without hindrance and without anyone knowing that he had returned.

His first thought had been to ride into Grover in plain view of everyone. But that would just scare Paxton off and though he might get his ranch back, he'd never again have the chance to finish off Paxton once and for all. Instead, Lee figured he would lay low for a couple of days and see what developed. By then Paxton might be convinced that Lee had not really returned and become emboldened once again.

In the meantime, he would pay a visit on Suzanne Clemons and try to discover precisely what was going on. That was the only good thing about Lisa's death. He could now unashamedly confront Sue without having to explain the girl. Though he mourned her passing, he knew Lisa would have been no match for the wild living that awaited her in Grover. And he would not have to face Lisa's mournful eyes every time she saw him walking through the streets with Sue.

Lee placed the crude wooden marker he had fashioned at the head of the grave and wiped his dirty hands on his jeans. The horses were still tied together in a chain of three, but did not seem to be in a hurry to start walking again. Lee made sure the ropes were secure and mounted the lead horse. He set out on a pace that would get him to town after dark and after most had retired for the evening. There would not be many people roaming the streets then and he would be able to speak to Sue in private.

Two hours later he was approaching Grover. Lee pulled the brim of his hat lower over his eyes and moved quickly along the back streets, weaving his way toward Sue Clemons' house. There was a light on in the window of what Lee Morgan knew was Sue's parlor, so she must still be awake. He tied the horses to the hitching post by the back porch and stealthily approached the window. Inside, he could see that Sue was sitting under a dim electric lamp reading a thick book. There was a wistful look in her eyes and Lee could tell that she was visibly upset about something. Maybe she would know more than he thought about what was happening at the ranch.

Lee tapped several times on the window with his fingernail and Sue nearly jumped out of her seat. At first she didn't seem to be able to tell where the sound had come from, but she was visibly frightened. Lee tapped again and Sue looked hesitantly at the window, wondering whether to investigate or run. Lee pressed his face close to the closed window so that Sue could see who was there. When she recognized his face peering inside, Sue had a horrified look as if she had just seen a ghost. Then came a look of relief and she ran to the back door, threw it open, and stared at the man still hunkered over beside her window. Lee immediately threw a finger to his lips, indicating that she should keep quiet and not give away his presence. Wordlessly, she ran to him and threw her arms around his neck. Then she broke away suddenly and indicated that they should go inside. The instant the door was shut they embraced again, Lee planting a much desired kiss on her warm lips. She pulled him onto the sofa and looked deeply into his eyes.

"What on earth happened to you?" Sue asked urgently. "You wouldn't believe what's happened since you disappeared."

"I'd believe it," Lee answered. "Fact is, I've already got a taste of some of it."

"Before I tell you anything else, Lee Morgan, you're going to tell me exactly where you've been for the last three months. Sam Lawton came to me right after you left and said you'd gone on some crazy expedition to Panama. How could you run off and leave your ranch unattended like that. What got into you, Lee?"

"I guess I ain't got an explanation that would make you forgive me for what I did. I just got an itch to do some traveling and thought it best that I leave before tears had a chance to flow. I'd planned to be back a month ago, but some folks had another idea. I'm lucky to be back at all."

"Not half as lucky as you think. Have you got any idea what's been happening out at your ranch? Rumors are flying everywhere. Everyone in town is convinced you're dead."

"I kinda figgered something like that. That's why I came here instead of riding through town this afternoon. I ran into a little trouble just south of Spade Bit and managed to hear Billy Paxton's name mentioned. You know there ain't nothin' in this world can rile me like the mention of that man's name." Lee was beginning to feel warm from the heat of the blazing fireplace and removed his jacket. Sue took the dusty garment and folded it as if it had just been freshly laundered. Lee leaned back in the couch, nearly exhausted.

"There's some leftover supper out in the kitchen. If you're hungry, I can fix you up a bite," Sue said, noticing how weathered Lee looked from his trip.

Lee's eyes brightened. "I ain't had one of your home-cooked meals since I left. I'd be grateful." Sue immediately disappeared into the kitchen. Lee thought that she had not changed at all. She was every bit as beautiful as she had been the day he left. Yet there was an odd weariness about her and her eyes looked very tired, as if she had spent long nights awake. Lee felt comfortable in her home. Sometimes even more so than he did in his own. All the feelings he had harbored for Sue suddenly came back to him in a rush. When she returned with the plateful of hot food, he came close to dropping to his knees and proposing to her on the spot. But he immediately thought better of it. Now was neither the time nor the place. Besides, after the untimely death of his first wife, Lee was going to have to think long and hard before he took another. He still was not over the pain.

Sue smiled at him as he devoured the hearty dinner. Lee had never known himself to be so hungry. He finished the meal within minutes and Sue was about to go back to the kitchen to get him a refill, when Lee swallowed the last mouthful and raised his hand for her to stop. "That's just about enough. I believe I'll have just a spot more tea to wash this down, then I want to hear all about what's been happening in town since I've been gone."

Lee could tell that Sue was not looking forward to this, but he knew he could rely on his friend to tell him everything he needed to know. Sue poured Lee another glassful of the sweet liquid, then leaned back next to him and waited for his questions.

"I've gathered that Callaway has called Paxton back in for another try at the ranch."

"It would seem that way," Sue sighed. "But to tell you the truth folks aren't quite sure just what is going on. Callaway and Deputy Chook have been making daily trips out to the ranch and that awful Paxton man and the fellows he's hired hang out at the Black Ace Saloon several times a week."

"What about my men?" Lee asked. "What's happened to all the boys runnin' the ranch? Why didn't they stop this?"

Sue didn't want to tell him, but she did anyway. "Most of them's run off, Lee. A few stopped in town on their way out. They looked like they had a good scare put into them, but there wasn't one would tell what was going on out there. Cain't say I blame them, either. Paxton's boys look like they'd kill for a glass of water on a rainy day. I imagine they intimidated a few of them into staying—at least those that didn't have no place else to go. Lee, please don't blame them. They were good men, but they weren't gunfighters. You can't expect them to lay down their lives for a man that everyone has given up for dead."

Lee felt a twinge of guilt at Sue's subtle accusation. But in his heart, he knew she was right. He should never have left the ranch, should never have gone on that fool expedition. And how could he harbor a grudge against men trained only to breed horses? "I never expected those men to look out for my welfare. I thought there was law here to do that."

"What are you talking about, Lee?" Sue chided. "You know what kind of law we have here. Did you really expect Deputy Chook to do anything? Why, he's one of the perpetrators! That young man named Sam Lawton rode into town one morning and told me he was going to Deputy Chook about the situation at the ranch. The next day he was thrown in jail for no good reason, and that's where he's been since. Chook won't let a soul in to see him and won't even explain why poor Sam is being held."

Lee looked astonished. "Sam's being held prisoner?"

"Yep. That's got folks upset more than what's going on at your ranch," Sue said.

"That boy wouldn't hurt a fly," Lee said. "Why isn't anyone doing anything about this?"

"Everyone's afraid, Lee. Paxton and his men have the whole town cowed. There's been some talk of breaking him out. But that's about all its been. Facing up to Chook is one thing, but standing up to a dozen professional gunmen is quite another."

Lee was suddenly saddened about how justice could be so corrupted even in this day and age. This was supposed to be a civilized world, yet bankers still worked their greedy schemes, gunmen still intimidated innocent citizens, and crooked lawmen still twisted the law as if the little parcel of land they watched over was their private property. Grover had been terrorized for weeks by these madmen who would own the entire town if they were able. And now that Lee Morgan was back it would seem that he was the only one able to do anything about it. And that's just what he was determined to do.

Lee took another sip of tea, then leaned back to let his supper digest. He had to think. The first thing he had to do was get Sam out of jail. That was simple enough. John Chook would be so spooked to see Lee stroll into his office that he would not only let the man out, but would probably offer to string himself up on the nearest tree. Chook would catch hell from Paxton, but what was he going to do about it? Lee figured that Paxton had guessed he was back anyway, but Paxton wouldn't admit it to anyone unless Lee showed his face to the townsfolk.

Once Sam was out, he didn't know what he would do, but whatever it was, it would be done quietly. And pretty much alone. Sam and Sue were the only people he could count on at the moment. That was like pitting two mice against a cat.

"Listen, Sue. I plan to break Sam out of jail tonight and I'm going to need your help. Seeing as my place is indisposed, how about letting the two of us hole up here for a day or two? Paxton won't risk molesting the town's leading female citizen, at least not right now. If he starts putting the pressure on, Sam and I'll hide out up in the hills. I'm going to need some time to put a plan together. It's be easy enough to ride to Boise and make sure the deed stays in my name, but if I do that, I'll never get Paxton. He'll vanish, just like last time when he ran out of tricks. You know I want him bad, and I don't intend to let him get away this time. He's going to face me, man to man."

"Oh, Lee, why do you always insist on trying to get yourself killed?" Sue said, exasperated at the thought of her man getting into another gunfight. "Can't you just inform the law up in Boise? If you tell the marshal what's going on, he'll be down here with an army of lawmen in a matter of two days."

"No!" Lee snapped. "I want Paxton for myself. He's responsible for the death of my wife, and I'm the one who has to make him pay. You can understand that, can't you?"

"I don't see the sense of it, but I can understand how you feel. I'd probably feel the same way if someone gunned you down in cold blood. Of course you and Sam are welcome to stay here as long as you like. There's plenty of room and you know I'd never pass up the chance to spend time alone with you."

"I'm obliged. Of course I'll pay you for the room and board . . ."

"Like hell you will. And don't you dare start getting formal on me, Lee Morgan. We've known each other much too long for that. Even if you did all but abandon me."

"You know I wouldn't abandon you. I just took a little . . . business trip," Lee said, almost stammering. "Now, look, I'm going over to pay Chook a little visit. I shouldn't be gone over an hour, but even if I am, I don't want you to worry. I'll leave the horses tied up around back and tap on the window again when we get back."

Sue looked wistfully at him. "Don't worry," she said. "I'll be waiting up."

Lee walked over and embraced her once again. He felt so stiff and awkward around her, but attributed this to the length of time he had been away. Being around her again would change this, he was sure. Even without his ranch he was already feeling like he was home again.

Sue opened the back door for Lee and he stepped out into the night. Immediately, he missed the warm comfort of her parlor and her soothing presence. Whatever had prompted him to leave in the first place would never overcome him again. Once he got Spade Bit back and Paxton out of the way, he was there to stay.

He checked the horses before setting out on his mission. After making sure they were secure, Lee grabbed his shotgun and loaded the barrel with two shots. Then he removed his whip and fastened it onto his belt. Lee stayed in the shadows all the way to the deputy's office, weaving in and out of alleys, avoiding the few people on the streets, wondering how he managed to get himself into these messes.

The jailhouse and Deputy Chook's office were so dark they could have been haunted. Lee approached warily, peering in windows as he moved toward the front of the building. Nothing was moving inside.

Lee stepped into the light from the gas lamps in front of the jailhouse, but stepped back into the shadows again just as quickly. There, leaning against the front door, half-asleep, was a man Lee had never seen before. One of Paxton's men, he guessed.

So, Chook was too cowardly to guard even one prisoner himself. Paxton had to assign one of his guns to do Chook's job for him.

Lee managed to slip back to the side of the building before the man could get a glimpse of him. This was going to be a little harder than he thought. There was no way Lee was going to get in to release Sam without first confronting the man at the door. But the fellow had looked half-asleep and this fact might work to Lee's advantage.

As quietly as he could, Lee removed his bullwhip from the fastening on his belt. Lee flung the woven leather weapon to its full length and watched the tip dance on the ground. This old friend had gotten him out of many a fix and now it was going to have that chance once again.

With his Colt in his left hand and the whip in his right, Lee stepped out of the shadows again and drew back the hammer on his pistol. The sudden click brought the guard out of his slumber and into action. The man responded by reaching for his gun faster than Lee had expected. Fortunately, Sue's meal and tea had pulled him out of his exhaustion. Alert as after a good night's sleep, Lee stepped forward and drew back the whip. He knew Paxton's guard had been instructed to not ask questions. He would kill any potential intruder as sure as he stood there. That way no one would dare attempt to free Sam, and Deputy Chook would keep his nose clean if there were any public outcry.

But the man fumbled with his sidearm an instant too long. Lee's whip lashed out and gripped the man's wrist like a single handcuff. In one motion, Lee jerked the man toward him and hit him in the head with the butt of his gun. The gunman opened his mouth as if to call for help, but he fell unconscious and his eyes rolled back in his head before he could make a sound. Lee was furious enough to cut the man's throat as he lay still, but decided that if he were to get his ranch back, being accused of cold-blooded murder would not look good for his case. He was going to have to do this as quietly as possible, without giving Paxton justification to do further violence.

Lee pulled a handkerchief out of his pocket and stuffed it into the unconscious man's mouth. He thought about tying the man's hands and feet, but without rope that would be impossible. Instead, he dragged the man by his feet around to the alleyway from which Lee had emerged. The man would probably remain out for a good long time, certainly long enough for him to pay a surprise visit to Chook, who by this time was in a very deep, secure sleep.

Lee returned to the front of the building and turned the door handle. He was surprised to find it unlocked until he got inside. There, on a small table beside the door was a pint of rotgut whiskey, three-quarters empty. That must have been the reason the guard had been so easily taken. Lee rested easier when he saw this. Surely the gunman would be out cold for the rest of the night.

Once fully inside, Lee gently closed the door behind him. Darkness returned to the large room as if someone had just blown out a candle. Lee waited a minute to let his eyes adjust to the dim light coming in through the few windows.

Then the thought occurred to him—what if Sam were not there? What if Paxton had gotten wind of Lee's return and had him moved back to the ranch, or worse yet, killed? Lee shuddered at the thought of what he might be moved to do to Chook and the guard outside if this were the case. Sam just had to be there, and he had to keep faith that he would be.

The jailhouse's two small cells, Lee

knew, were at the back of the building, and Chook's cot would be in an even smaller room before he got to them. Lee tucked his whip away and walked on his toes to the back, being careful not to awaken the man before he could surprise him. Lee heard a sound and stopped dead in his tracks, his gun at the ready and hoping his eyes had adjusted well enough to allow him to shoot straight. But the sound had only been snoring, and his hearing told him that the drone was coming from more than one man. So Sam Lawton was still there.

The door to Chook's quarters was ajar and Lee stepped stealthily inside. The man was laying on his back and appeared to be sleeping fitfully. Lee almost felt pity for the man. Chook didn't have an inherently evil heart, but he had chosen the wrong profession for a man of his spineless constitution. He should have stayed in New York where he had come from and taken over his overbearing father's business. But Chook could not tolerate his father's manner and customers' constant demands on him so he had fled west to make a new life for himself. He had answered an advertisement in a newspaper for a deputy to look over the town of Grover, and thought that it would be a good chance for him to make some good money and a name for himself. But things hadn't turned out quite as he had planned. Once in office, more people were making demands on him than ever. He was expected to settle disputes and keep the peace—not an easy task in a town as wild as this. No wonder the marshal had so readily hired him on. They would have taken anyone. He hadn't been sworn in two months before the banker had started requesting special favors. At first they were simple but annoying tasks, like looking over the bank while he was away on business. And those favors had soon grown into looking the other way whenever Callaway cheated someone out of a trifling amount of money. And now this . . . Chook had no idea how he had gotten involved in taking over a man's ranch, but he knew there was nothing he could do about it now, especially with Paxton and his men giving the orders.

Lee leveled his gun at the sleeping man's chest and struck a match on the sole of his shoe. Chook stirred and rolled over onto his side as Lee touched the lighted stick to the oil lamp on Chook's writing desk, and Lee guessed that he was not going to have any problem with this man at all. He could probably steal the deputy's keys, open the cell and clomp loudly out to the jailhouse without even waking the man. But he was not willing to take that chance.

The room was now filed with an eerie dim light, casting shadows of Lee onto the wall and making him appear even larger than life. With his right foot, Lee kicked the deputy's cot to wake him. Chook snorted and pulled the blanket over his head, causing his bare feet to stick out the other end. Lee kicked again and suddenly the cot was a mass of thrashing blanket.

"Who . . . What?" Chook stammered, trying to fight his way out of the binding blanket. "What's going on? What do you want?" he went on, still looking for daylight.

Lee bent down and picked up the holster laying by the cot, then placed it on the desk near the lamp. "Get up, Chook. It's time you and me had a little talk about your future in this job."

Chook recognized the voice immediately and violently flung the blanket from the cot, his eyes wide with terror at the sight of Lee Morgan standing over his bed with a gun aimed at him. "Mr. Morgan," he managed to say. "You're supposed to be . . ."

"Never you mind what I'm supposed to be. Fact is I'm here. Funny thing is, so are you. You knew good and well I'd be back and so did Paxton. I really didn't think you'd have the guts to stick around with that on your mind."

"But the guard . . ."

"Don't you worry about him. He's sleeping sounder than you were. He ain't gonna make a peep. Probably don't even know what hit 'im."

Chook sat on the edge of the cot and slumped his shoulders in defeat. He should have known Morgan would be back and should have run when he got word that he was. Now Morgan had him dead to rights and after the last fiasco with the Spade Bit ranch, he'd be lucky if Morgan let him live. "Well, kill me if you're gonna," Chook sniveled, bowing his head. Then he muttered, "I shoulda never left daddy's factory."

Lee had not planned on killing the man, but the thought had sure crossed his mind. He would have thrashed the man senseless right then if he had not felt so sorry for the coward. Instead, Lee slapped the surprised Chook across the face. "Get up and get your goddam pants on, you little shit. Look at you. You're supposed to be a lawman, but you won't lift a finger less someone's pointing a gun at your head. If I had any sense at all, I'd do you a favor and pull the trigger right now. But I'm not that nice. You're going to do some good for folks whether you like it or not. Now get dressed."

Chook had no idea what Morgan was talking about, but he stood, pulled on his pants and tucked in his night shirt.

"What do you want me to do?" he asked.

"Some cooperation, for starters. You're going to do just what I say and maybe, just maybe, you'll get the chance to redeem yourself. You screw up and Paxton's gonna be draggin' your sorry ass from the back of his horse all the way back to New York."

With a look of near panic on his face, Chook realized that he didn't have much choice at the moment. If he did as Lee asked, his name was mud as far as Paxton was concerned, Paxton would chase a man to the end of the earth to get revenge. The fact that he was back to get even with Morgan was proof. But, then, he didn't want to overestimate Morgan's kind heart either. Either way, he would probably not come out ahead, but for the moment Lee Morgan held all the cards.

Who were the riders after me on the ridge this morning?" Lee snapped at him.

"I don't know," Chook whimpered. "Couple of men Paxton sent out to patrol the border in the hills."

"Names," Lee demanded, shoving the barrel of his gun against Chook's neck.

"Honest, Morgan," Chook said, trying to twist away. "I don't rightly know. He's got over a dozen hands up there, none of them I've ever seen in these parts before. From their voices, I'd guess they were from the south but I can't be sure. The one who brought back the dead man is called John something or other. The other two I don't know.''

Lee removed the gun from Chook's head. "I guess it don't matter right now," Lee said. "I'll find out soon enough. Where's your keys?"

"Keys? What keys?" Chook said, not understanding Morgan's meaning.

"The keys to the goddamn cells, you idiot! Do you think I came here to have tea and cookies with you? I want Sam Lawton out of here tonight!"

Chook looked at Morgan with admiration. The man had quietly arrived in town mere hours ago and already he knew what was happening at his ranch and that Sam Lawton was being held. Morgan was efficient if nothing else. But one thing Chook was certain Morgan didn't know was how he was going to get his ranch back from the banker who would hold the whole town hostage to get the land. And what did Morgan mean that Chook was going to have the chance to redeem himself? Did Morgan really expect him to stand up to Paxton alone? Morgan might as well kill him right out if he did.

"Look in the desk drawer," Chook said. "Your man's in the first cell down the hall."

Lee stepped to the door of the room and took a quick look down the hall. There was no sign of anyone stirring. "Open the drawer and take the keys out. Then get down the hall and open that cell."

Chook sensed that this was a test, but Lee was looking for a chance to give him what he deserved. Lee was still looking out the door while Chook walked over to the desk where the keys were tucked away, but on the top of the desk was the holster and pistol Lee had earlier placed there. Lee was giving him a chance to go for the gun, testing his willingness to do as Lee asked. Chook thought that he might have made a play and might have even gotten off a shot, but if he did, Morgan would show no mercy. It wasn't a chance he was willing to take. Morgan would be expecting him to make a move. Chook removed the keys, picked up the lamp, and walked past Lee's smirk and through the door.

Lee gestured for the man to lead the way down the dimly lit hallway, taking time to glance toward the front door, as if he expected the guard to come bursting through, guns blazing, at any moment. Lee should have felt exhilarated over having gotten this far without detection, yet he felt strangely depressed over having to go through this ordeal at all. He'd been in tight situations many a time, but for the first time he almost didn't care whether he won or lost this battle. But then he thought of Sam and Sue and how they would be depending on him. Lee was the closest thing to law and order Grover had seen since before Chook arrived.

The lamplight and the clanging keys woke Sam out of his slumber. He sat quietly up in his bunk as if he had been awake all along, expecting Paxton to come for him in the middle of the night to silence him forever. When he saw Lee Morgan step out of the shadows, a big grin covered his face and he rubbed his eyes in disbelief that his friend and employer had finally come home.

"Evenin', Mr. Morgan. I was starting to think maybe you wouldn't get back in time." But Lee could tell that Sam had never doubted that he would return to save the day.

Chook silently unlocked the door and let the bars swing open. Sam was out of bed in an instant and shaking Lee's hand with enthusiasm and gratitude. Chook just wondered what was going to happen next. Morgan couldn't very well let him go, and even Morgan wasn't ruthless enough to murder a lawman in cold blood. If he did that, he'd never see his ranch again.

"Give me them keys and go sit on the bunk," Lee demanded.

Chook did as he was told and watched as Lee locked the gate again with Chook inside. "So you're just going to leave me locked up in here all night?"

"What would you have me do? Let you go so you can run back to Paxton? If I did that, Paxton would know you helped me and I let you go. He'd kill you for sure. Like I told you, I'm giving you a chance to make good. And if I don't see you trying, I'll be the one to drag you back to New York. The keys'll be back in the drawer."

"What about me?" The voice came from the second cell. Lee looked surprised to hear Luke Bransen's voice. He looked to Sam questioningly.

"Paxton's guard brought him in this afternoon," Sam said. "Guess he figured since you were back in town he might be more trouble than he was worth. Deputy Chook here's been boasting about how Paxton has run off all your men. They kept Bransen to show them how the operation works and because he was too drunk half the time to stir things up. I came to Deputy Chook when the trouble started just like you said, Mr. Morgan. I didn't know he was involved with them or I'd have gone straight to the marshal in Boise."

The man in the cell looked sober enough. "You all right, Luke?" Lee asked. "You been hurt?"

"I'm just fine. And I'll be even finer when you let me out of this rat trap."

Sam took the keys from Lee and opened the door. Lee had gotten more than he had bargained for. As much as Bransen liked to drink, Lee valued the man's assistance. He knew every inch of the ranch—probably better than Lee himself—and that knowledge might come in awfully handy in a pinch.

"I'm forever grateful, Lee. Ain't nothing more distasteful than the inside of a jail cell." Bransen picked up the few personal belongings Paxton let him keep and hurried out of the cell, slapping Lee on the back on the way out. "Good to see you're alive, Lee. I was beginning to wonder if what everyone was saying was true."

Lee smiled at the man's spunk. Bransen was the only one of his hired men he allowed to call him by his first name. None of the others dared to address him as anything other than Mr. Morgan. Bransen hadn't changed a bit. Though several years Lee's senior, he managed to retain his youthful enthusiasm for life. That alone had gained Lee's respect. If Bransen's drinking were the cause of his self-assurance, Lee was going to have him hit the bottle at the earliest possible date.

Sam reclosed the cell door and the three men headed for the front door without so much as a goodbye to Chook. Chook, however, was too busy worrying about how he was going to explain this to Paxton to think about it. Lee took a second to toss the keys back into the drawer then followed the other two into the night. It seemed a lot colder now and from the dampness in the air Lee knew that it would not be much longer before the first snowfall dusted the range. He was worried about the well-being of his animals. Bransen would have managed the ranch without a hitch throughout the winter, but Paxton would know nothing about horses except how to ride one. Without proper attention, Lee's prize horses would be in pitiful shape come spring.

And then there was another worry. Lee had obtained Sue's permission to stay over with Sam for a night or two, but what was she going to say when he showed up with Sam and Bransen? Though harmless, Bransen was not the most couth of men. On numerous occasions Sue had commented to Lee about the man's unruly behavior in town. Bransen's drunken binges were known throughout town. Taking him to Sue's place was a chance he had no choice but to try.

There was still no one on the street to see them, but as the trio rounded the corner into the alley, Lee was stunned to see that the guard he had knocked out cold was staggering to his feet. Still without arms, Sam and Luke took a step back, not knowing that the guard had no gun either. The guard instinctively went for the gun that was no longer there, then his eyes turned white when he gripped air. Lee stepped forward with something in his hand, and the two former prisoners thought for a second that Lee was going to put the man out of his misery.

"Please . . ." the guard said, terrified, and threw his arms in front of his face to ward off his fate. "I didn't mean nothing. I was just doing a job . . ."

And then Lee shoved the whiskey bottle into his hand.

3

She was not amused. Three men in her house—and she had wanted to spend the evening alone with Lee his first night back. But she said nothing. She was even cordial and ladylike with Bransen. And he had remembered to remove his hat when he entered her home. She should be grateful, she reasoned, that Lee now had another man loyal to him in his time of need. Lee was going to need all the help he could get against Paxton's cutthroats.

After the men had eaten the snack Sue had prepared, and Lee had checked on the three horses one final time for the evening, Lee said they ought to be retiring. They would have to get up early in the morning to make plans for the recovery of the ranch. Lee still had no idea how he was going to get the ranch back and finish off Paxton, but maybe a good night's sleep would give him a brainstorm.

Sue left for her room after giving Lee a slight peck on the cheek. It was less than Lee had hoped for but more than he expected given the circumstances.

Sue had a small, but cozy home, one that most of the women in town were envious of. That was but one of the reasons she was shunned by most traditionalists, men and women alike. Headstrong and progressive minded, Sue was involved in varous causes most felt women had no place even discussing, much less participating in. And that was what had attracted Lee to her in the first place—her ability to stand up for herself, and others not as fortunate as she. Not to mention that she was the most goodhearted, most beautiful woman Lee had ever had the pleasure of knowing. She was such a stabilizing influence that Lee found himself wishing that he had met her years before.

Lee slept fitfully. The two men he had broken out of prison began snoring as soon as their heads hit their pillows. Twice he got up to throw a fresh log on the fire, and each time he went to the front window, pulling back the heavy tapestry-like curtain to get a clear view of the street.

This wouldn't do. He was so nervous Paxton would somehow find out he was staying in the Clemons house that he considered staying up to keep watch all night. But as he lay back on the cot Sue had set up for him, the heat from the hearth and the droning of the mens' snores finally lulled him off to sleep.

The next morning he awoke to the smell of bacon frying and coffee brewing. For a moment he didn't know where he was, but then he saw Sam and Luke sitting on the couch sipping the steaming coffee and remembered all the troubles awaiting him in the day ahead. He wanted a bath more than he wanted breakfast, but decided that that could wait. There were more important things on his mind than either.

The heat from the wood-burning stove in the kitchen made it warm enough so that the main hearth did not have to be relit. Yet Lee still felt a chill.

"Have some coffee, Lee," Sam said, taking another sip from the mug he held with both hands. "Sue says she'll have breakfast on in a few minutes.

Luke nodded his affirmation, wishing that he had a bit of whiskey to spice up the coffee.

Lee groggily got to his feet and rolled up his bedding, then went to the kitchen without a word to either man. He wiped the sleep from his eyes while Sue poured him a cup of hot black liquid and then went back to the main room with the two men.

Lee hardly knew what to say, but the men looked on anyways as if waiting for Lee to reveal some dark secret. Even Lee himself was wondering what he would say.

Finally, after burning his lips on the coffee, he put the mug aside and began to speak. "I know you men think I expect you to help me out of this jam. You know Paxton and Callaway have taken over my farm, and you both know I plan to get even with Paxton no matter what the cost. If you two want to scoot on out of here right now, I won't hold it against you. I didn't break you out expecting any favors, but you don't know how grateful I'd be if I could count on your assistance." Lee gave them both a long hard look and waited for their reply.

Sam and Luke could see Lee's desperation. Sure they could leave, and probably find jobs up in Boise, but Lee had always been a fair man and deserved more than that. "I'm staying," Luke said right away.

Sam hesitated a moment and then said, "Mr. Morgan, you've always done right by me. You gave me a chance when I didn't have a job, and I appreciate that more than anything."

Lee looked at the man sympathetically, knowing that he was about to bow out of

Lee's plans, but he let Sam continue.

"I don't much care for violence," Sam said, "and I know there's going to be plenty of it. But I don't care for folks throwing me into jail for obeying the law, either. You can count me into whatever you have planned. I ain't much of a match to Paxton's hired guns, but I'll do my best to help you get back your ranch."

Lee smiled at the man's devotion, and he realized that, despite his past misgivings about Luke Bransen, he had in his presence two of the finest men he could have hired. "As I understand it Paxton has about a dozen men guarding the ranch . . ."

"As of yesterday, he's got ten," Luke cut in, referring to the two scouts Lee had killed on the ridge. "Now that he knows you're back, he's likely to send for more. Paxton's a sly devil, but beneath all that he's also a coward. He wants you dead more than Callaway wants your land, but he won't stand up to you alone. He'll get all the support he can to back him up. We're going to have to make our move fast if we're to stand a chance."

"Which means we've got about two days if he's bringing in men from out of state. Even without them, the job's going to be next to impossible. Thirteen against three ain't such good odds, but I want you to know I appreciate your staying to help me." As he finished, Sue brought in the first tray of food and placed it on the dining table, and the three men wasted no time meeting her there. Fresh scrambled eggs, grits, biscuits, gravy, and crisp bacon tantalized their noses and started their mouths watering. Sue was pleased to know that her efforts were appreciated, and she hurried back to the kitchen to refill the quickly emptied trays. When she returned, she sat down to get a bit for herself before the feast vanished again.

"We've got three good horses," Lee was saying. "I've got a couple of spare side-arms and a rifle for each of us. Ammunition's no problem. Plenty of rounds in the packs I brought in last night. And thanks to Sue here, we got a place to stay for a night or two. It ain't much, but it'll have to do. I may have put enough of a scare into Chook last night to get some help from him, but I wouldn't put any money on it. Right now he's probably on his way to given Paxton the dirt on what happened last night. He'll get a good chewing out, but Paxton's smart enough not to cause any problems with the law, especially when it's working for him."

Lee went on. "The only way we're ever going to get the ranch is to split up Paxton's men, and I'd be willing to bet that's going to happen this morning. Paxton will send men in to town sometime this morning to look for us, but we're going to be on our way back to Spade with a little surprise of our own. I only hope that Paxton is there so we can get this over with fast. But even if he's not, we'll stand an even chance of reclaiming the place."

Sam looked up from his meal, excited by Lee's pep talk but with a dread that could only come from realizing that he might be riding to his death. "Even if Paxton does send half a dozen men into Grover to look for us, that's still going to leave another six at the ranch. Think the three of us can handle them?"

Lee understood Sam's concern, but stood his ground. "I'm mounting up right after breakfast. You can still back out if you want to and no one will call you a coward if you do. Six men ain't so bad if we catch them by surprise. 'Sides, if we give them a good enough scare they might run off before the shooting starts."

Now it was Sue's turn to worry. "You think Paxton will come here looking for you?"

"It's likely he'll come here right after inspecting the jail. Callaway's sure to have told him how close we are. Just make sure this place's cleaned up real good. Don't leave a trace of us out in the open. And if he starts asking questions, play dumb. Like you don't know what he's talking about. He's not likely to push you too far."

As soon as the last mouthful of breakfast was finished, Lee and his two-man army went out back to inspect, saddle up the horses and pack the few belongings they had brought inside. Lee made sure that each mount carried a rifle with plenty of spare rounds in the saddlebags. He handed both men a sidearm, which they tucked into their belts since Chook had relieved them of their holsters at the jail. Together they looked more like a band of rustlers than ranchers.

Even though he had a full night's sleep, Luke Bransen looked as if he had already fought a war. He hadn't had a drink in two full days now, and was beginning to get a bit jumpy. Lee saw the man staring vacantly and when he called out his name Luke's hand visibly twitched as if to draw. "Luke—you all right?" Lee said, more than a little concerned.

"Yeah. Just a little shaky is all. I ain't been in a fight like this since the war. Guess I've just got the jitters is all."

"You ain't got a thing to worry about," Lee reassured him. "You're the best damn horseman in these parts, and Lord knows you can shoot. Just make like those thieves back at the ranch are empty whiskey bottles and you'll be okay. Just because they've got more guns don't mean they've got more sense.''

"Sure, Lee. Sure," was all Luke could say.

But Lee was beginning to worry about the man. He must have been under considerable strain since Paxton and Callaway took control of the ranch. From what Lee could gather from Sam, the two schemers had offered to let Luke stay on to manage the ranch until the deed was transfered to Callaway and the land was divided. Though Luke was still loyal to Lee, with no place else to go, he had reluctantly agreed to their proposal, all the time drinking more and slipping closer to uselessness. By the time Paxton expected that Lee had returned, there was no longer a need for Luke, Paxton had simply had Chook haul him off in a stupor to wait out the happenings in jail with Sam.

Usually Luke was a jovial, but unpredictable man. Now Lee saw within him a deep depression that only a renewed clearheadedness had allowed to show through. Luke had proved himself to be still loyal to Morgan, but it was evident that he was embarrassed that he had not done more to protect Lee's land when the trouble first started. Lee now sensed that Luke's shame was quickly being replaced by a deep-seated rage—directed both at

Paxton, for having taken advantage of him, and at himself, for not having the guts to stand up and fight when he had the chance. Now he had his second chance, and he was not going to let this opportunity to repay Paxton get away from him.

Lee considered letting his presence be known by riding down Main Street through the center of town. Luke and Sam had been released and the community's support might help along his cause. Besides, if Paxton were going to run, he would have done so at the first hint that something might go wrong with Callaway's plan. He changed his mind when he thought about how that act might lead Paxton to suspect that Sue had somehow collaborated with them. Her life might be placed in danger, and the death of another woman—especially Sue Clemons—was something he did not want resting on his shoulders.

The three men set out in full gallop, riding wordlessly, each wrapped up in his own fury over the men who would destroy their lives for a small plot of land. They headed north at first, but once well off the trail and away from Grover, they circled to the West and the well-worn road that led from town and eventually to the trail that would take them to Spade Bit and the revenge they desperately sought. They reached the trail without being recognized, and slowed to a walk so as to be alert to any approaching riders.

After his fitful night of sleep and thought, Lee was grateful for the brisk, cloudless morning. The cold air rushing past his face brought his full attention to matters at hand. He tipped his wide-brimmed hat back to get a panoramic view of the surrounding territory. It had been too long since he had taken this old trail, and the memories of those frequent trips into town to visit Sue only steeled his resolve to defend his right of property. He suddenly remembered the two sticks of dynamite in his pack. He hadn't told either Sam or Luke about them because he didn't intend to use them unless he was forced to. Still, he would not hesitate to blow up the ranch house if he thought destroying the building would destroy Paxton as well. The thought of rebuilding the ranch house a third time in as many years was not pleasant, but if he allowed Paxton to escape this time, he would never again spend a restful night.

Sam brought him out of his musings with a shout and an outstretched hand. "Mr. Morgan! Look up ahead there. Just over them trees . . ."

They had just come to the top of a rise out of a mile-long stand of pine. Ahead of them was a sloping decline that descended for another mile with no cover except for the dense grass that seemed to stretch forever down the slope on either side of the trail. Beyond that was a smaller stand of hardwoods where Lee and Sue had often picnicked. Beyond that was what had gotten Sam so feverish—a large cloud of dust swirling like a twister in the morning breeze. There were Paxton's riders, coming directly and furiously toward them. The trees and raised dust kept Lee from seeing just how many of them there were, but from the size of the cloud, he guessed there were at least the six he had expected would come to town looking for them.

From his vantage point at the top of the rise, Lee appraised the situation. The riders obviously did not expect to meet any resistance on the way to town, and it was equally evident they were very much in a hurry. Lee had seen signs that a rider had preceded them to Spade Bit earlier that morning, and had guessed that it had been either Chook or the guard Paxton had assigned to the jail. In all likelihood it was Chook who had remained in town—perhaps still locked in the cell where Lee had left him to think about his misdeeds.

At any rate, there was not much time for preparation. If Lee and his two men were still in the open when the riders broke through the trees, they would be seen for certain, and if that happened they would not stand a chance against the larger approaching party.

"Turn back," Lee said calmly to the two stunned men. Surely Lee was not running away after they had come so far. Had his trip to Panama left Morgan afraid of a fight?

The two men did as they were ordered, but understood Lee's intentions when he motioned that they should enter into the stand of pines. Far from running from a fight, Lee had strategy in mind. Dismounting, they led their horses deep into the underbrush, calmed them, and made sure they were securely tied. If any of them were to scare, Lee's position would be given away and the fight would be over before it started.

They returned to the main trail and, chancing a peek over the rise, Lee saw that the men were over half way up the side of the rise. They would be upon them within minutes. Lee could not afford to waste another moment. He took up a position behind one of the broadest pines and made sure his rifle was fully loaded. The other men followed suit. Beads of unnatural sweat popped up on Sam's forehead and Luke's damp hands shook violently.

"Keep low and keep quiet," Lee whispered in warning. "Don't shoot until they're right alongside us and you're sure you can get off a clean shot. Don't panic and we'll have them beat—or at least half of them. If Paxton's with them, he's mine.''

The three crouched in the underbrush and thistle, their six eyes focused on the spot where the riders would breech the top of the hill, wide with anticipation. Then they heard the hoofbeats where it had moments before been silent. Lee prayed that the riders would not stop for a breather at the top of the hill. As fast as they were traveling, Paxton's men were not likely to spot the additional hoofprints until it was too late. But it would take only one sharp-eyed gunman to turn Lee's impromptu ambush into a disaster.

The first horseman breeched the rise like a demon from hell, the rider hunched behind the animal's neck, the horse blowing hard, steam billowing from its flaring nose. If they intended to continue riding at that pace, the horses would be dead long before they reached Grover. Lee wondered if he was so important that these men would kill their mounts to catch up to him. Then he realized that these were his own horses Paxton's men were abusing.

Renewed anger swept over him as he watched the riders come over two at a time. There were seven in all—more than he had anticipated. They were all heavily armed, but did not act as if they were expecting a fight. They were about to ride right past the trio hiding in the brush when the second horseman reined to a halt, pointed to the ground, and yelled back. It was Billy Paxton.

The regulator had spotted the maze of hoofprints Lee's men had left. Lee wasted no more time. The other riders were reining in and bunching around Paxton to see what he was pointing at. Lee took steady aim at Paxton's head as the outlaw followed the tracks with his eyes. When Lee was confident that Sam and Luke had also drawn a bead, he gently tensed his finger on the Remington's trigger and felt the gun buck solidly in his hand as the bullet left the barrel.

But Paxton's head was no longer where it had been. He had stooped to inspect the hoofprints just as Lee fired, thus fouling Lee's aim. At the sound of the shot, and the two following, Paxton's head jerked up as if someone had hit him with an uppercut. But he just as quickly turned to see the man beside him. Callaway Jones, his best man, had been hit square in the face by Lee's misplaced lead. The man was slumped over his horse, unable to scream. His hands had momentarily covered his face when he was hit, but were now hanging limp at his side, dripping warm blood on the trail. Paxton didn't have to give the man a second glance to know that he was beyond hope.

Paxton's hands immediately went to his sides and leveled with a pearl-handled pistol in each. Three of his men had fallen, one with a bullet in the side of his head and another lay on the ground dying as blood filled his punctured lung. Still, he could not see who his attackers were, or where they were shooting from. But one thing he knew for certain: Lee Morgan had fired that first shot. With only four men left, Paxton wanted to get out of there in a hurry. He had no idea how many Lee had with him, but now was no time to stand around and count heads.

With shots hitting all around him and nothing to shoot back at, Paxton did the same thing any other rational man would have done—he jumped on his horse and kicked its flanks with a spur, urging it back into a full gallop. The other three surviving members of Paxton's gang had already beat him to the idea and were several lengths in front of him, running for their lives from their unseen enemy. None of them had even bothered to fire back.

Luke broke through the brush despite Lee's call to stay put and began firing wildly at the fleeing horsemen. Paxton turned just long enough to see Bransen taking aim, then ducked as the slug whizzed past his head and into the back of the man directly in front of him. The man arched backward as the bullet tore through his body and out his chest. It was as if the man's heart had simply exploded. When the man fell from the horse, Paxton didn't even bother to look back.

Luke ran to make sure the fallen man was dead and then returned to the other three bodies where Lee and Sam were now standing, gaping at the carnage. Lee rubbed his grizzled face with the palm of his hand while he thought about what to do next. Once again he had failed to get Paxton and he was sure now that Paxton knew he was a hunted man, he was going to be more careful. For now, Paxton would have to make do in town with the two men he had left. Lee had succeeded in dividing the group. Paxton would not be able to show off his muscle in Grover now, and Lee was sure that Chook's loyalty to the man would be eroded even further once he learned of the travesty Paxton had just walked into. The men left at the ranch now had no leader, and without that to hold them together, Lee's task would be much easier.

"Luke," Lee said. "Go back up the trail and rope that miserable carcass you shot to his mount and bring him back here." Luke gave Lee a puzzled look but understood that Lee was not to be questioned. He turned immediately and backtracked to where the man lay. "And keep your eyes open," Lee reminded him. "Those fellows might make another run through here to get back to the ranch." But Lee knew that this wasn't going to happen. Paxton was probably most of the way to Grover by now.

"Sam," he went on, "help me get these bodies back on their horses. I want 'em sitting tall."

Now it was Sam's turn to give Morgan a curious look. "What do you mean to do, Mr. Morgan?" Sam asked hesitantly, hoping that Lee wouldn't snap his head off for questioning him. "We ain't gonna take them with us, is we?"

Lee's rage had not died down one bit. "Even dead, I wouldn't give this scum the pleasure of riding with me. I'm fixin' to give those boys back at the ranch a scare like they've never seen before. Just get them loaded up like I told you and you'll see what I'm blabbering about."

Together the men tied the bodies to the saddles one by one, their legs fastened to the stirrups and their wrists tied to the horn so that none of them could slip off. Then Lee tied the horses together so that they formed a chain. Sam thought for a moment he was going to be sick at the sight of the four bloody corpses mounted on the steeds. But neither man questioned

Lee's motives. They both knew the horrors Paxton had brought upon Lee in the past, and even if they didn't approve of Morgan's brutal methods of getting revenge, at least they were willing to go along with him.

Lee gave the horses a final look over, then walked to the lead horse and slapped the animal smartly on the rump. The horse shook its head violently, then took off in a trot back down the rise toward Spade Bit and home.

"You think they'll go back to the ranch?" Luke asked.

"Where else are they going to go?" Lee asked rhetorically. "Them's my animals they were riding. They know where home is, and that's where they'll go, if for no other reason than to get those bodies off their backs. And when they get there, those men are going to have something more to think about than overseeing a ranch."

"What do we do now?" Sam asked, sitting on the ground and inspecting his rifle.

"Exactly what you're doing," Lee replied. "We sit and wait. I figure it'll take about an hour for them horses to make their way back to the barn. The ones that aren't scared off ought to be easy pickins." Lee walked back to the top of the rise and surveyed the horizon. He had stood here so many times before he could point out the exact tree above which the smoke from his ranch-house chimney would rise.

Perhaps it had been profane to desecrate the men they had just killed in such a way, but it also occurred to him exactly what was at stake. It wasn't just Spade Bit that mattered, it was, in the long term, the livelihood and safety of the entire community. They had worked so hard to build civilized lives on a frontier that was even wilder now than before the white man came. If Callaway and Paxton were allowed to have their way now, they would be bolder in the future. Everyone in the county would consider that even their land might not be safe. After all, Callaway ran the bank and held all their money for safekeeping. Would he insist on calling all the shots as well?

The hour went by slowly, and the men passed the time smoking and chewing on the pieces of jerky and pemmican Sue had packed for them. Though the midmorning sun was soothing and the air invigorating, the three were none too comfortable about sitting in the middle of the trail where they might be attacked themselves. Every few minutes, one of them would go again to the top of the rise and look out to see that there were no more riders approaching. In the dense stand of pine and needles, the horses were finding little to eat and soon began giving indications that they too were ready to move on.

At length, Lee spoke: "There can't be more than four of them down on the farm. Seeing as we just killed four of 'em and three more are in town, that can't leave more than four if you counted right, Luke. Their bodies we sent down are gonna put the fear of God into them, but it's also going to keep them on their toes. They'll be looking for us. So were going to have to circle around and approach the ranch from the west. There's a thick stand of trees there that'll provide cover and a place to leave the horses . . ."

Once again Sam had to wonder what this once sane man was getting them into. Did Morgan really think they could just walk in and take the ranch without a fight? Lee had already alerted Paxton's henchmen that something was up. Now he was going to lead them into the midst of four professional gunfighters, all of whom had every reason to want them dead.

"We're going in on foot?" was all Sam could manage to blurt out. "In broad daylight?"

"Would you rather that we ride up to the front porch and give them a few howdy-do's?" Lee joked. "Maybe we could bake them a couple of pies to show how hospitable we are. Fact is, they'd blow us off our horses before we got within a hundred yards of the place. Now, I don't know about you fellows, but I'd prefer not to get caught out in the open."

Sam silently conceded that Lee was right, especially since he was in no position to argue. It was Lee's ranch, and Sam had agreed to come along for the duration. He'd never be able to hold his head up again if he backed out now.

"If there are no more objections, we'll move out now," Lee said, rising to his feet and dusting off his trousers. The three men remounted their horses and let them trot to the bottom of the hill. Paxton had shown no sign of returning and the way seemed clear.

Once they reached the trees at the bottom, they turned north to make the long circle around to the west side of the property. Though it was still early morning, the chill had gone out of the air and the horses heated easily.

Spade Bit was only two miles away, but Lee Morgan still had a long way to go.

Once they reached the main road, Paxton and what was left of his party reined to a halt and spun around to check the trail behind them. They had run as if stampeding for well over a mile. The horses were ready to drop and the riders were not in much better shape. Paxton and his two men had managed to escape injury, but each was visibly shaken over the surprise attack.

"God damn it!" Paxton screamed, throwing his hat in the dirt and trying to keep his mount calm. "How the hell could I have been so stupid?"

The other men had dismounted to give their tired horses a deserved rest. If not for them, they would all be dead for sure.

"Bushwhacked by a son-of-a-bitch ranch hand with a rifle. I knew I should have left another guard in town." Paxton looked like a frustrated general as he sat high in his saddle and let his horse prance around the other two men. He was naturally prone to violence and could strike fear into the heart of even the bravest of men with his icy stare. Now, even his own men were beginning to wonder if he might ever turn on them in his anger.

Billy Holmes looked into Paxton's reddening face. "It wasn't just Luke shooting back there. You heard all them guns. Sounded like a damn shooting gallery. We didn't even get off a shot. I still don't know where they were shooting from."

"I wonder how long they'd been hiding in them woods," Callaway Jones added, still out of breath from the wild ride.

"You can bet Morgan and that goody-two-shoes Lawton fellow was right there with him," Paxton went on, fuming, "and now they're probably on their way to the ranch. Those boys down there better keep alert or Morgan will have them picked off one by one."

Holmes and Jones looked at the man as if he had lost all his senses. "We were going to town to find Morgan," Holmes said, "and now you know that he's heading for the ranch. Why the hell aren't we going after him? Between us and the fellows back at the ranch we can take 'em easy. What's gotten into you, Paxton?"

Paxton jumped off his horse and ran up to Holmes with his fists clenched. Holmes backed off immediately.

"Are you going to keep on questioning my decisions, or do I take your head off right now?" Paxton's eyes were bulging out and his face had become as red as his hair. "What the hell makes you think Morgan ain't still hiding out in the woods? For all we know he's got half the town with him. Morgan ain't just fast with a gun. He's smart, that Morgan is. He's got something up his sleeve, and we're not rushing into nothing without getting our advantage back."

"But what about the ranch?" Jones attempted to argue once again. "Callaway ain't going to like this."

"To hell with Callaway." Paxton said, calmer now. "You're working for me, not him. And you'll do as I say. I don't give a hoot about the ranch. It's Morgan I want, and I aim to get what will hurt him most. That's why we're still going to Grover."

There was nothing left to say. They would have to let the horses rest, but within a half hour, they would be on their way to town again. Jones and Holmes were still not sure why, but one thing was for certain, they had signed on with Paxton and it was too late to back out now.

Far from the show of bravado they had originally planned in town, the mood had turned to one of melancholy. Paxton's rage had diminished and his face was now set with a look of quiet determination. As the three men rode through the center of Grover, all heads turned their way. It was unusual for Paxton to show his face in town without a large detachment of armed rowdies. Almost everyone on the street, from playing children to proselytizing merchants, stopped what they were doing to gape at the lathered horses. Instinctively, they knew there must have been some trouble, but no one dared ask what it was. Usually when Paxton made one of his infrequent trips into town, it was to pay a call on Callaway's bank. But this time he rode right past, dismounting only when he had reached the stark jailhouse.

Paxton and his men hastily tied their

mounts to the tether and let their horses drink deep from the stale murky waters of the trough in front. They wasted no time getting inside, and the town's citizens wasted even less time going about their business.

From the cell where he had been sweeping one of the jail's stone floors, Deputy Chook heard the front door open and the sound of several sets of feet shuffling inside. With an overwhelming sense of dread he stopped what he was doing. He knew it was Paxton before he heard the man's voice. Chook had been expecting a visit all morning, and now his time had come. His first thought was to lock himself inside the cell he had been cleaning out, so that Paxton could not get at him, but that would be futile and would get Paxton even more riled.

Chook stepped out of the cell and into the hallway holding his head as high as he was able considering the circumstances. He didn't dare smile, and when he encountered the scowling faces in the front office, he could hardly hold back the tears.

"I don't even want to hear your miserable excuse for letting this happen," Paxton breathed in a voice that froze Chook in his boots. "Just tell me how many Morgan's got with him and I might just let you live."

"I-I-I don't know. J-just the three of 'em was all I saw. I was dead asleep when Morgan came in. He had a gun on me. Threatened to blow my brains out if I didn't let Lawton out. There wasn't nothin' I could do. He had the drop on me. The guard . . ."

"Shut up! I said I don't want to hear your lame excuses. I give you a simple little job to do. Just watch over two men—locked in a cell yet, and you still fuck it up. I don't know what marshal in his right mind would give you a goddam star, but I do know I ought to blow a hole through that tin badge right now. Morgan didn't have anyone with him? He just walked past the guard outside and past you, and nobody even fired a shot at him?"

All the courage Chook had tried to muster had vanished under Paxton's brutal interrogation. His head drooped and his jaw hung almost limp. "That's about how it happened," he managed to say in a voice just above a whisper. "If Morgan had someone with him, I didn't see him. He might have had some help taking out that guard, but if he did, the other fellow stayed outside."

"Help taking out the guard?" Paxton chided, looking back and forth between the two men who had come in with him. "The only thing that took out that guard was a solid punch in the jaw. He was too drunk to even know what hit him. Why the hell did you wait till near morning to come and tell me what happened?"

"Well—uh—Morgan sort of locked me in the cell before he left. I sent the guard as soon as he woke up. Looked like he'd been drinking a lot last night."

"Locked you in the cell, did he? You'll be lucky if I don't lock you in a pine box before this is over with. Do you have any idea what this has cost me?"

Chook stammered and twisted the broom handle in his sweaty hands. He braced himself for the worst. If Paxton didn't shoot him dead right then and there, he would be the most grateful man on earth.

"This whole scheme is falling apart because of your bungling. Morgan and those sorry ranch hands you were supposed to be looking out for ambushed us this morning on the way in. Four of my best men are dead, including Callaway Jones, the only man I've got besides me who could have outdrawn Morgan in a fair fight. And now he's dead with a bullet through his head. Morgan's headed for his ranch and if they don't get stopped there it's gonna be his again, and everybody in town will know what we've been up to."

Chook was stunned that Morgan had acted so fast. He didn't think Morgan still had the old fire in him. So, it was really Paxton who was lucky to be alive. Maybe it was time for Chook to rethink whose side he was really on. After all, he had been trusted with a badge and all that it stood for. Still, this was no time to make a stand for law and order. "Have you been over to tell Callaway?" Chook ventured.

"I don't give a good goddam whether Callaway gets that ranch or not. I got all the money I need. You think I came all the way back here to help out poor ol' Mr. Callaway? You must be even stupider than him. I'm back here for one reason only, and that's to put Morgan six feet under. It took me a year to build back my reputation after word got out about that last fiasco with him. There's still people saying I shot his woman in the back. I can't help it if some confound farmer gets carried away with a rifle and I can't help that she got in the way. But Morgan still blames me, and will until I make him shut up for good.

"So, Chook, should I kill you or give you another chance?" Paxton finally said. "I still aim to get Morgan. There's no way I'm runnin' now that I've come this far. 'Sides, if I did, he'd probably come after me. I'd be willing to bet he's just as determined as I am."

Chook's eyes widened at the thought of being tortured by Paxton, and he could not force himself to respond. He wished now that he were back in New York, in a nice easy job, pandering to his father's customers and staying out of trouble. What had he gotten himself into? No matter what he did, he would lose. If he did Paxton's bidding, either Morgan would kill him or he would lose his job. Even if Paxton ultimately got his revenge, the regulator would probably decide to kill him anyway. But if he stood up to Paxton, he would probably end up dead even sooner.

"Well, Chook, I'm going to count on you one last time. If you fail me, you can count your prayers. I've still got one ace left to play, and if that don't break Morgan's bank, nothing will." Paxton's eyes narrowed as his idea took form.

"Are you going back to Spade Bit?" Chook asked. If Morgan had really retaken the place, Paxton and his two sharpshooters would hardly stand a chance alone, and help was still well over a day off. He would have to try a different tack. And soon. Word would soon spread of Morgan's return, and once that happened, even the town's citizens might take up arms against Paxton.

"Spade Bit's the last place I want to see again. I aim to make Morgan come to me." Paxton was working himself into a frenzy again. He was acting more like a little kid who had just won a game of kick the can than a violent man bent on revenge. Was this man becoming unglued in his single-minded determination to kill a man everyone in town respected? And how did he intend to get at Morgan with his men dead and no one except Callaway on his side? Callaway's influence, except for what his money could buy, was nonexistent. Though respected for his position, Callaway's bank held nearly everyone's savings and the exorbitant interest he charged on loans to homesteaders certainly won him no friends.

"What do you want me to do?" Chook asked, hoping it wouldn't be much. People had been grumbling about the way he did his job, rather the way he didn't do it, for some time. Working in such close association with Callaway, and now Paxton, a known criminal, had people wondering whether their town was really safe.

"I want you to do exactly what you were doing when we came in. Just clean the offices and go about your job as if nothing were unusual. The boys and me are going over to pay our respects to Mr. Callaway and tell him what his trusty deputy let happen last night. We'll be gone about an hour, and when we get back, I'm going to want you to run a little errand for me—one that involves delivering a little message to Mr. Morgan."

Chook didn't like the sound of this. Callaway would hit the ceiling when he heard Paxton's version of how Chook ruined Callaway's last chance to claim Spade Bit. Callaway might even take up a gun himself. And what did Paxton mean about delivering a message to Morgan?

"What sort of message you got in mind, Paxton?" Chook asked nervously. He prayed that this ride out to Spade Bit was not going to be his last.

"A message that'll have Lee Morgan back in Grover before you can say Jack Robinson. I'm plannin' to be waiting for him with something he wants real bad."

"Only thing I can think of that he would want that bad is Spade Bit. And it looks like he's probably already got that," Chook said.

"You're forgetting Suzanne Clemons," Paxton said, and his broad smile revealed a golden tooth.

4

The leaves in the grove of trees to the west of Spade Bit had turned a luminescent orange in the late September sun. Winter was likely to arrive earlier than usual, for in the shade the morning's frost had not yet thawed. Still, out in the open it was as warm as a spring day, and by the time Lee and his two hands reached the cover they had shed their denim jackets and were ready for another rest.

Lee rode between the other two men through the trees, pointing the way to the stream that led to the trout-filled pond at the back of the ranch house, even though Luke and Sam probably knew where it was better than he did. The tired horses thirstily sucked up the cool, quick-moving water while the men walked around to stretch their aching legs.

The scene seemed incongruous with the task at hand. Lee reminisced in his mind about the many times his father, the famed gunfighter Frank Leslie, had taken him fishing in this stream when Lee was a boy. It had been his father's dream to retire from the limelight and raise his son in quiet seclusion, the way a son should be raised, away from the vileness of the world and in the midst of the greatest gift God ever gave to man—nature.

But like father, like son, Lee had been restless and set out with a reckless determination to make a name for himself at the first opportunity. Lee suspected that his father secretly never forgave him for this, though no harsh words were ever exchanged between them regarding Lee's hard living. At least his father had not been ashamed of him. Lee had won a reputation as a master gunfighter, but both father and son knew Lee was never in a fight unless it was for the right reason. Lee earned his notoriety, but he was no criminal, and was always as straight and strong as the oaks he was now sitting under.

Frank Leslie had worked hard in his autumn years to transform Spade Bit into the finest ranch in Idaho. People came for hundreds of miles to inspect and purchase Leslie's fine breeds, and from just as far for the chance to stud their mares with his choice stock.

But that was all very long ago. After Leslie's death, the ranch fell into disrepair, its reputation slumped, and the surrounding acreage was taken over by the hordes of sodbusters looking for the chance to find a new life in the green hills of Idaho. Spade Bit sat all but idle for years—until the day Lee Morgan found love, money, and a desire to settle down.

For him, Spade Bit was going to be a chance at a second life—a life that would not be filled with mindless killing and an endless stream of women and whiskey. Lee Morgan had changed, but the times were not changing with him—at least not fast enough. There had been one threat after another—from Wilson, from Paxton, from the farmers who coveted his land enough to kill his wife to get it. And finally from himself, as he wrestled with the idea that maybe he was not cut out for the life of a gentleman rancher. Maybe that was why he cut out for Panama without so much as a goodbye.

But now that he was back, he knew he had been wrong to leave. Paxton's threat to his property had convinced him that his father's legacy was more important to him than his freedom. And then there was Sue Clemons. That she loved him, he knew from the day they had first met, even before his wife had been killed. But until that tragic event, he never dared admit his feelings about her. She would make a fine wife, a wonderful mother. He was on the verge of asking her to marry him before he left, but now that he had returned, he was not sure that she still wanted him. The pain of being abandoned had had a grevous effect on her, and although they had not yet talked about it, he knew that it would take some time before all wounds were healed.

Right now, however, Lee Morgan had more pressing things on his mind. His home had been invaded once again and there would have to be much bloodshed before he could get it back. Even in the west, where men moved to live free from the bonds of the "civilized" east, there was still enough injustice to move an honest man to tears.

For Lee Morgan this was no time for crying. It was a time for fighting. There were four men between him and Spade Bit, and that was four men too many. He would have to take care of his unfinished business with Paxton later, there were more important matters to attend to at the moment.

"I think we've rested just about enough, fellows. This is going to be dirty work, not to mention dangerous, so let's get it over with so we can rest easy."

Sam and Luke knew what he meant. They both went to their mounts and began removing the packed gear. "Leave 'em saddled," Lee said, "just in case we have to ride outta here fast." And as soon as he said it he wished he hadn't. Losing this battle was a possibility, but he sure didn't want to give the only two men he could count on the idea that they might have to run.

Each man loaded his six-shooter and tucked a dozen more bullets in their shirt pockets so they could get at them easier should the need arise. They would have to do most of their fighting with the rifles, but there was always the chance of a close encounter. The three repeating rifles were loaded to their fullest, and boot knives were freshly honed.

They were to carry nothing more. The rest of the gear was stowed out of sight in the underbrush of the stream bank, and the horses were loosely tied to a low hanging branch of a young oak.

"By now they've gotten the message we sent down off the ridge," Lee said while cleaning the barrel of his gun. "They're gonna be expecting us, but they sure know we mean business. Before we go in I want both of you to remember, these fellows earn their livings with their guns. I don't want to give them a chance to start shooting if we can help it. You see one, you shoot to kill. Chances are that they're not as handy at long range as they are with their sidearms, and it's a good bet that once they spot us they'll all head for the ranch house. They'll have cover in there, but once they're in there, they won't be able to run anywhere but into us.

"I want you two boys to wait at the edge of the woods and cover me good. I'm going to make for the barn and let the horses out to pasture. We'll have 'em trapped then. They'll have to come out to us sooner or later, and when they do, we'll have 'em."

As they came within sight of the ranch house, Lee couldn't help but notice how quiet it was. There was no sign of any other human being. Even the birds were still—as if they had cleared out in anticipation of the upcoming bloodshed. The big red hangar of a barn stood some fifty yards off, just to their side of the house. Though anyone looking out of one of the house's upper windows would surely be able to spot him, he doubted that they would be able to do anything to stop him. He would be behind the barn before anyone inside even had time to shoulder a rifle.

Lee didn't say another word, but sprang out of the cover to the brush and sprinted toward the structure where he hoped his treasured horses would be waiting. As he hit the dirt behind the barn, he was surprised that no one had fired a shot. Perhaps they still did not know he was there.

Lee put a small door into the back of the barn when he rebuilt it the year before, after the Jack Mormons had set a torch to it. The door was intended to be a means of escape should the barn ever burn again, but right now, it would make a perfectly good means of entry. Lee gently pulled the door open a crack and peered into the dark, musty interior. There was no sound except for the easy nickering of the horses in the stalls, and the only light came from the narrow gaps and the knotholes in the planking where sunlight hesitantly streamed inside.

It was enough for Lee to see to let the horses out of their stalls and push the main door open. Lee had been expecting at least one of the men to be posted in the barn, but there had been no one. He did find, however, the four horses he had sent to the ranch with men on their backs. The bodies had been removed, but evidently, the men in the house had not wanted to take the time to remove the horse's saddles. Once Lee had opened the door, he slapped one of the horses and it bolted for the opening. The other animals followed suit, running through the yard toward the open pasture.

Then the shooting started. Lee barely had time to duck away when the first bullet bit the dirt by his feet. That was followed by another that shattered the

planking of the wall Lee was hiding
behind. Lee guessed that the men were
firing from the upstairs window of the
house. There, they would have an
overview of the surrounding grounds, and
a clear shot at anyone approaching the
building. These men were professionals,
yet they had missed him while he stood in
the open. As he ran to the back of the
building and the door through which he
had entered, Lee couldn't help but wonder
whether sending the dead men back to the
ranch had made the men inside reconsider
his temerity.

As he reached the back of the barn, Lee
noticed that Sam and Luke had already
begun returning fire to the second story
window. Gesturing frantically, Lee
indicated for them to stop. Firing blindly
into a now empty window would do them
no good. Lee was going to have to rely on
his wits as much as his skill with a gun to
flush the men out. And, failing that, he
always had the two sticks of dynamite. He
only hoped that he was right in guessing
that Paxton would not return without
additional help.

Instead of running back to the cover of
the woods, Lee held his position by the
barn. With all four men inside the house,
Lee's chances were much better. At least
he would know where they all were. Now
he would have to position Sam and Luke

on either side of the house to split up the four men inside. He waved Sam over to him and Sam sprinted the distance without incident. No more shots came from the upstairs window.

"Sam," Lee said. "I want you to get inside the barn and keep this side of the house covered. I'm going to try to position Luke behind the big oak in the front yard. That way you can keep them busy, we'll have two sides of the house covered, and they'll all stay in one room. I'm going to try to pick my way to the back of the house without being seen. There's an opening there that leads to a crawlspace under the house. From there I can come up into the kitchen and be on top of them before they even know I'm in the house."

"Whatever you say, Mr. Morgan. We're behind you all the way," Sam answered.

"All you fellows gotta do is stay out here and keep their guns busy for a few minutes. Think you can handle that?"

Sam couldn't believe that this was all Lee was asking him to do. He hoped Lee did not misunderstand his smile as he nodded his head. They might just get out of this alive yet.

"Just keep the bullets comin' till I get in there. You'll know I'm there 'cause they'll stop shooting at you and turn to me. As soon as they stop, you and Luke make for the front door. And make it quick, 'cause

I'm liable to need your help fast. Got all that?"

Sam nodded again and stepped inside the barn.

Lee whispered again, "As soon as you get into position, fire off a couple of shots so I can get back to the woods. And once I'm there, keep 'em busy till Luke can get to the tree. If he doesn't make it, we're both up the creek. Now, give me your pistol."

Sam looked at Morgan questioningly but Lee quickly explained. "You ain't going to have any need for it down here, but I'm sure as hell going to need it up there." Sam passed him the loaded weapon and emptied his pocket of shells. Lee poured them into his shirt pocket with his own. Lee caught his man's eye and for an instant he felt the unbounded admiration Sam held for him. "Good luck," Sam said shortly, shaking Lee's hand. And then he disappeared into the barn.

When Lee heard Sam's first shot, he took off as if a pack of arctic wolves were right on his heels. He was halfway to the woods when the first shot whizzed by his head, almost punching a hole through his best and only Stetson, and when he dived into the bushes with shots flying all around him, he nearly lost the thing altogether. Had Luke not joined Sam in returning fire, Lee almost surely would not have made it the rest of the way. But now was not the time to stop for thank you's. Lee joined Luke where he hid and pointed to the broad, leafless oak in the front yard. Luke knew what he was going to have to do, even before Lee explained. He frowned at the idea of having to run thirty yards in the open, but Luke knew that unless he did, there was no way Lee could get inside.

"Sam and I will cover you the best we can. Just weave in and out between the saplings and you'll make it easily," Lee said, trying to muster the most reassuring smile he could. But Luke saw through it and read the desperation etched in Lee's eyes. Without any acknowledgement of Lee's words, Luke stood and began to run with all his might straight for the tree, not even bothering to dodge bullets as Lee had suggested. He had gone almost ten yards before Lee even knew what had happened. Lee had to rush to get his rifle shouldered. He was able to get off one shot before Luke was spotted. Two men began shooting at him, firing as fast as they could cock their guns. Slugs shot up dirt and divots of grass all around him. It looked as if there had been a group of boys skipping stones in a lake of green all around him. Except these stones were made of steel and were coming with enough speed to shatter a man's leg or burst his skull.

Luke was now within the radius of the tree, with its near naked outstretched arms, but the browning leaves on the ground slowed him, making Luke lift his legs higher as he approached the trunk. The men inside were now ignoring the shots fired by Sam and Lee. They had a chance to hit a man in the open and were taking full advantage of the opportunity.

Lee saw what they were up to and also saw an opportunity. He stopped firing wildly and took careful aim at a bearded man in the window. As if an accomplished buffalo hunter, Lee took his time and gently squeezed the trigger. The gun jumped in his hands and Lee saw the man disappear from the window. He couldn't tell whether he had hit the man, but at least he had stopped shooting. When Lee turned to look for Luke, he, too, had vanished. But there had been no place to run, nowhere to hide but the tree.

Lee was just about to look *in* the tree when he saw the leaves begin to stir down below. Then Luke's head popped out of the midst of the crinkling mass. *Safe,* Lee thought. *He's made it.* But as the rest of Luke Bransen's body emerged from the pile of leaves, Lee saw the blood and saw that Luke was clutching his left arm. From the expression on Luke's face, Lee could tell that the man was in a great deal of pain. All at once Luke dropped to his knees and began thrashing about wildly, throwing leaves every which way, flailing like a mad dog. Lee thought the man had gone insane with the pain of his wound. Though Luke was still behind the tree, if he didn't get himself under control he would end up with another bullet through his chest. But the man had not gone crazy. His hands finally found the gun he had been looking for. He swept it up, made sure the barrel was not clogged with dirt, and held it up to his good shoulder. Positioning himself against the tree for support, and wincing in pain at having to use his wounded arm to steady the barrel of his rifle, Luke began firing into the open window nearest him, causing the men inside to momentarily duck out of sight. Lee didn't waste another second. He ran back into the dense cover and out of sight.

Lee hoped that Luke and Sam would be able to keep up the heavy fire while he circled around to the back of the house and put his chancy plan into action. If even one of the gunmen inside began to wonder what had happened to Lee, he could end up dead and Sam and Luke would have to flee for their lives.

The back of the ranch house seemed a different world, almost peaceful except for the gunfire coming from the front. Getting inside was going to be easier than he thought. Breaking from the cover of the trees, Lee ran to the back of the house and crawled between two rose bushes, ripping his plaid flannel shirt as his back scraped against the low thorned branches. He crawled on his elbows on the ground against the house until he reached the entrance to the crawlspace. All he had to do was open the hinged plank in the wall and crawl inside. Then he saw the lock. Someone must have anticipated someone gaining entry this way and put a padlock on the small door. It might have even been Luke or Sam trying to protect the house from intruders. And now it stood in his way of throwing the intruders out. Lee's heart sank as he looked around for another way inside. But unless he went in through the window, there was no other way. And if he broke the window he would be heard for sure.

Lee crawled past the small door and lay on his back listening to the shouting out front. He was going to have to do something soon. Sam and Luke had plenty of ammunition, but the men inside would soon realize that Lee had vanished and begin to check the other sides of the house.

With the heel of his trail-worn boot, Lee kicked at the padlock. Nothing happened. After two more sturdy kicks he thought he felt it give a little. Maybe this wasn't going to be so impossible after all. Lee drew his leg back and gave it a kick that could have knocked a horse out and the lock pulled free. Lee was able to twist the metal plate holding the lock with his bare hands and pull the door free. It opened just wide enough for him to squeeze his body inside. Once there, he pulled the door shut behind him. If someone were to look out the window, nothing would appear disturbed without closer inspection.

The dank, musty smell of moldy earth hit him immediately, the staleness of it almost forcing him to gag. It was as if he had dug his way under a cemetery. There was no light and Lee had to struggle in the confining space to reach into his pants pocket for a match. He lit the thing on his belt and held it aloft to get his bearings. Green, glowing eyes seemed to scatter everywhere as September's field mice scampered to hide from this unlikely intruder.

Lee had to crawl almost the length of the house to the kitchen entrance. Nails sticking through the door clawed at his back, forcing him to stay on his belly. The match burned low and Lee thought it best to drop it and use both arms for crawling. It fizzled into the damp earth and Lee moved on blindly, feeling his way past the support post holding up the house, stopping to wipe the spiderwebs from his face. When he had completely lost his bearings again, Lee fished out another match and struck it on one of the posts.

He had aimed himself well. There, ten feet in front of him was the square outline of light that would lead him out of this cold wet hell and into a hell of another sort—one far worse than anything Satan had ever devised.

Lee wormed the rest of the way to the opening and tilted up the trap to peek inside the once spotless kitchen. For a moment he wondered if it was his own kitchen. Spoiled food sat on every counter. Empty whiskey bottles were strewn all over the floor. Boxes of provisions were stacked up against every inch of wall space. Lee wondered whether the animals were living in the barn or in the house.

Opening the trap door to its fullest, Lee stood and pulled his body into the kitchen. His clothes were wet and filthy from the ground under the house, and his hair was coated a white mass of cobwebs. If he didn't kill the men upstairs, he would at least send them into a helpless fit of laughter.

The shooting upstairs had slowed somewhat. Lee heard commands and obscenities being shouted and there was a lot of stomping about in the room just above him. Luke and Sam had not stopped firing. For a moment Lee was tempted to put the dynamite in the rafters over his head and be done with the whole thing. Saving the house didn't matter so much now as killing the men who would take it from him. At least that way there would be no chance of his men outside being hurt.

But that might be too foolish. Lee himself could be killed and Paxton could sit in the Black Ace Saloon and gloat over his victory and over Lee's grave. Callaway would get his land and he would put his father's name to shame. There was just nothing to do but force himself up the stairs and confront the four gunmen—and pray that Sam and Luke got inside the house to back him up.

Lee checked the loads in the Colts and held them both at the ready as he inched his way on his toes to the stairs at the main entranceway. The men were in the room at the far end of the hall, and although over the gunfire and yelling they were not likely to hear him, Lee wanted to make sure they were taken completely by surprise.

Dropping low, Lee made his way up the stairs on his knees and one hand. Still holding the guns in both hands, he was careful not to take his eyes off the hallway where one of the men might come running at any time. At the top of the stairs, Lee peered around the edge of the railing he had so lovingly worked on the lathe in the barn. He had a clear view of the window facing the barn and Sam. All he had to do was shoot the two men standing on either side of it. He could have killed them from where he was, but that would have been too easy. He wanted them dead, yes, but he wanted to make sure they knew just who their killer was.

While the men were still occupied, Lee stood and walked directly to the doorway, a gun trained on each of the two men. He stood there framed like a picture for nearly a full minute until one of the men turned to reload.

The man's jaw dropped when he saw Lee Morgan, unable to move in his wonderment over how Morgan had gotten inside. When his mouth finally began to move in warning, Lee shot him through the chest. It was as if someone had suddenly come up behind the man and jerked him by the collar. His arms shot out to his sides and his entire torso flew backward through the window, sending blood, shattered glass, and bits of wood falling through the air. Lee hoped that that would be enough of an indication for Sam and Luke to make their move.

The other man in the window witnessed his companion's fall and turned quickly to confront their attacker. He hadn't even raised his weapon when Lee put a shot into his head, sending him flying against the wall, his hands clutching at the gaping wound between his eyes. The man was oblivious to the fact that the back of his skull no longer existed.

The shooting had stopped altogether. There were still two men inside the room, shielded by the door behind which Lee stood. They were staying quiet, perhaps trying to guess Lee's next move. Out of the corner of his eye, Lee saw that, aside from the man he had just killed, the four bodies he had sent down on horseback were stacked neatly in a far corner. The men he was after hadn't even taken the time to bury the corpses, preferring to hole themselves up in a room with the bodies until Paxton arrived with reinforcements—help they had not realized would never come.

Lee could hear Sam and Luke entering and then climbing the stairs. Sam ran to join him but Luke stayed at the top of the stairs. The men behind the door had not yet made a move or a sound and Lee was beginning to wonder if maybe he had miscounted them. He had just stepped back to consult with Sam when the three bullets tore through the door where he had been standing. Lee's temper snapped. In an instant he was in the room and firing round after round, not even bothering to look for his target. He was beyond caring now. If these people were going to take his father's homestead, so be it, but they were going to have to do it through a wall of gunfire.

Lee was hitting nothing—because there was nothing there to hit. A dead man lay on the floor. Lee guessed it was the same man he had shot while Luke was running to the tree. There was a gunshot wound through his gut and more blood on the floor than Lee thought a human body could hold.

The whole scene in the room was one of carnage. Blood was everywhere, broken glass was strewn all over the floor and on the bodies, and no one but Lee Morgan was breathing.

But where was the other man? Lee had been sure there were four. There was a sound outside like scraping metal, and Lee realized that the last gunman, the man who had shot at him through the door had escaped through the window. Lee ran to the shattered window and knocked out the rest of the frame. Bloody footprints marked a path to the end of the tin porch roof. The man had slid down one of the porch supports and was now running at a breakneck pace for the horses grazing a half mile away in the pasture.

Lee turned back to Sam, who was staring open-mouthed at the pile of bodies they had killed earlier. "Give me your rifle, Sam," Lee said calmly.

Sam didn't take his eyes from the dead men, but handed his rifle to Morgan. Lee snapped it out of his hands and went back to the window. He aimed and fired one shot, which shook Sam out of his trance, then tossed the gun back to Sam.

"That about does it," Lee said.

Sam fell to his knees and began to wretch. The gruesome sight had been too much for the young, inexperienced man to take. Lee left Sam in his misery and went to check on Luke's wound. Luke was sitting at the top of the stairs with his head between his knees, almost as if asleep. Lee shook him and slapped him awake. Luke had been unconscious and was still losing a lot of blood from his left arm. Sitting like a child waiting for its mother to bandage a scrape, Luke watched the blood ooze down his arm and drip to the hardwood floor from the tip of his finger.

"Sam!" Lee hollered. "Sam, quit your gagging and get over here. Luke's hurt bad." Lee lay Luke back on the floor and tore off the sleeve of his shirt, gently pulling the soaked fabric away from the wound.

In the bedroom where the gunsmoke had barely settled, Sam pulled himself together and wiped his mouth with his shirt. Wishing he had something to wash out the bad taste in his mouth, Sam got to his feet and joined Lee in the hallway. When he saw Luke's pallid face and the gaping gash in his arm, Sam thought he was going to be sick all over again.

Lee's anxious voice and a slap across the face brought Sam to matters at hand. Luke might be bleeding to death, and it was up to him and Lee to do something to save him.

"It's okay, Mr. Morgan. I'm all right now. Is he going to be . . ."

"I don't know," Lee said. Luke was unconscious again and looked as white as a two day old corpse. "Looks like he's in shock. First thing we gotta do it get him into the bedroom. Grab his legs."

Sam did as he was told and the two men carefully moved Luke's still body into the bedroom at the other end of the hall. They covered him with as many blankets as they could find, and Lee sent Sam downstairs to the kitchen to boil some water and scrounge up some clean kitchen linen.

Lee wiped as much of the blood away as he could and discovered that the injury was not as bad as it had originally seemed. There was no permanent damage to the man's arm, just a good sized chunk of flesh torn away. If Luke had had it attended to immediately after being shot, he would not be in the state he was in right now. But as the bleeding had not been checked, Luke was on the verge of death.

Lee held his handkerchief tightly against the man's arm to stop the bleeding until Sam returned with the water and cloth. Sam had also brought back part of a bottle of whiskey he had found.

"Good man," Lee said, hoping to reassure Sam that, though he had snapped at him, he was not angry.

Lee cleaned the wound as best he could and Sam uncorked the whiskey and almost took a slug for himself before handing it to Morgan. "It's a good thing he's unconscious," Lee said. "I'd sure hate to be awake and have this stuff poured into a sore. Hurts worse than salt." Lee turned the bottle over and let the contents sterilize the gash. Then he soaked a piece of cloth with it and placed it on Luke's arm. With a long section of toweling, he wrapped Luke's arm and returned it under the blanket.

"Shouldn't you tie a tourniquet," Sam questioned, remembering the first-aid manual he had been required to read in grammar school.

"He don't need it," Lee said. "He lost a lot of blood out there by the tree, but it ain't that bad. 'Sides, if I did, he'd most likely will lose that arm, and that's the hand he pours with." Lee's attempt at levity had no effect on Sam, who was still too awed by Lee's doctoring abilities to understand what was meant.

"We've got him wrapped up pretty good, but he's got to stay warm." Lee got to his feet and Sam followed him downstairs and out to the woodshed for a few logs to get a fire going in the upstairs fireplace. Once the fire was blazing, Lee went alone to the barn.

There were dozens of holes in the side of the barn and enough in the barn door itself to tell what was going on inside without opening it. Lee looked back at the house and was almost sorry he had not dynamited it. It was in such sorry repair from the month of abuse and neglect Paxton's men had put it through that Lee would not have recognized it as his own if here were not standing there looking at it with his own eyes. Shingles were coming lose on the roof, the porch steps were broken, the yard was a sea of broken bottles and trash, and finally there was the room where Lee and his men had lain siege against the four murderers holed up there. Lee had won this battle, but there was still a war to fight.

Guilt was beginning to set in. Had he been wrong to coerce Luke and Sam into helping him? This was not their ranch, and Lee had no right expecting them to help him defend it. Yet they had, and without them Lee would probably not be back home at this moment. And though Paxton's hired guns were not going to be causing anymore trouble, the cost had been Lee's nearly losing one of his best friends. If Luke did not recover, Lee would never be able to face himself again. His would be a hollow victory.

Inside the barn, Lee walked to where the tools were stored and took a spade and pick off the wall. Lee threw them over his shoulder and walked back out into the brilliant sunlight. He looked again at the pock-marked second story of the house he had rebuilt just a few short months ago, then walked slowly back to the front of the house.

"Sam," Lee shouted through the upstairs bedroom window, where Sam was sitting with Luke, "get out here. There's a lot of digging to be done."

Suzanne Clemons was worried sick. Though she knew Lee Morgan was fully capable of handling himself, she couldn't help but wonder how he would fare against the vicious gang Billy Paxton had put together. Lee had a good deal of experience in such matters, but with three men pitted against a dozen, his chances didn't seem to be very good. Sue had prayed for his safety that morning—and prayed even harder that the whole matter could be resolved without anyone getting hurt. Why didn't Paxton just go away and leave the God-fearing people of Grover alone? What had they ever done to him?

Sue had cleaned the breakfast dishes and put them away, and had moved the rest of Lee's belongings to the attic where they would not be seen should someone drop in unexpectedly. She had followed Lee's instructions perfectly, but was not sure that she could keep his secret much longer. She longed to run out into the street and tell the world that he had returned, that he had survived his trip to Panama after all. Surely the town would rally to Lee's defense if she did. They might form a posse to ride out to Spade Bit and confront Paxton's men.

Sue shrugged her shoulders and brought herself back to the real world. Who was she fooling? Sure, folks might be happy to hear that Lee was back, but this was a bustling town. People were much too busy with their own concerns now to get involved in someone else's problems. Especially if shooting might be involved.

How she wanted to march over to the bank and announce Morgan's return to Jesse Callaway in a voice loud enough for everyone to hear! She wanted to blame him, to chastise him, to force him to face the fact that his greed had been the cause of all the town's problems. Callaway wasn't good enough to make it as a banker back east, he had to come out west and use his conniving ways to swindle honest folks out of their hard-earned pay.

But that wouldn't do either. Callaway would just laugh at her, and the people in the bank would think her even more pixilated than they already did. There was nothing to do but follow her regular routine and hope that Lee returned soon.

She took a broom out of the kitchen pantry and mindlessly began sweeping the floor, angling the nonexistent dirt into the center of the room. She was so deep into her daydream about how she could help Lee that she didn't notice the strange face peering through the window at her.

Paxton and his two surviving men had walked from Callaway's bank to Sue's home so as not to attract attention in the street. As long as they seemed to be behaving themselves, people didn't care where they went or what they did. Even so, there were still a few eyes that followed them suspiciously down the main street.

Once they got near Sue's place, Paxton posted one of his men in the street in front of her house, then went around to the back with his other man. He knew that once they got inside Sue would put up little resistance. There would be no way she could fend them off, and with as few friends as she had, there would be little likelihood of any neighbors dropping in. Paxton's only problem would be getting her back to the jailhouse without arousing suspicion. If Suzanne Clemons were seen riding or walking with him, it would cause quite a stir in town.

The knock at the back of the door startled Sue out of her reverie. She wasn't expecting any visitors and no one would come around to the back door to enter, except Lee . . . She ran to the door and swung it open expecting to greet her lover's smiling tanned face. The face that greeted her was smiling and tanned, but it didn't belong to Lee Morgan.

"Good afternoon, Miz Clemons, beautiful day, ain't it?" Paxton said, the pleasant smile never leaving his face. He was dressed completely in black and seemed an imposing malevolent figure standing in her doorway with his hands poised on his hips.

Sue gasped and stepped back, taking the door in both hands to slam it in the intruder's face. Paxton took a step up and placed his foot firmly against the door, causing it to bounce back when she swung it. Another step up and Paxton was inside her house and standing just a foot away from her.

Suzanne's first thought was to run as fast and as her legs would carry her, run somewhere where she would never have to see this man again. She backed up a step and turned to make for the front door. But as she did, Paxton's massive hand clutched her wrist. There was no escape now. She wondered if he planned to kill her now or rape and torture her first. If she screamed, no one would hear her cries. Her house was set well off the main street.

"That's no way for a lady to greet a gentleman caller. Did you slam the door in Morgan's face as well?" Paxton was asking through the devil's own smile. Sue felt the blood rush from her face and her legs suddenly turned to gelatin. Even Paxton was surprised when the woman fell in a dead faint at his feet, his hand still clasping her wrist.

After Paxton carried her to the parlor couch, he sent the man who had accompanied him to the front to give the all-clear sign to the man in the street. As they entered through the back door, Paxton was hovering over the woman, waving a small bottle of smelling salts under her nose.

"Is she hurt?" Winston asked him, seeing the unconscious woman for the first time. "She ain't dead, is she?"

"No, she ain't dead," Paxton answered. "Now shut your trap and both of you search the house. Make sure there ain't no one upstairs."

Just then, Sue began tossing her head back and forth to get away from the overwhelming vapor burning her nose. Paxton removed the salts and brushed her blonde hair from her face. Suzanne's eyes shot open as if in surprise, then darted wildly about the room, trying to fathom what had happened to her. When they finally rested on Paxton's looming face, she turned pale again and her eyes rolled into her head. Paxton, who had been holding her hand, felt her grip go limp in his palm. Without trying to revive her again, he placed her hand by her side and covered her body with the afghan draped over the back of the couch. Then he replaced the cap on the bottle of salts and set it on the table beside him.

As he sat back in the easy chair to think about what to do about this new development, Wilson and Kelly came plodding down the stairs. "Ain't nothing or no one up there, boss," Kelly was saying. Then seeing Suzanne still prone on the couch. "What the hell's ailing her? She sick or something?"

Paxton stroked the grizzled stubble on his chin for a moment, never taking his eyes off the woman. "Damn!" he swore. "Just like a woman. I don't know what Morgan sees in a woman with a constitution like fine china. She just one look at me and passed out like I'd poured a bottle of liquor down her throat."

Both Wilson and Kelly snickered but their poker faces returned when Paxton shot them a malevolent glance. Paxton went on with his story. "She woke up for a second, then passed right out again when she realized what had happened." Paxton sighed and leaned forward with his elbows on his knees, his palms pressed against each other and against his lips.

Wilson and Kelly walked to the woman and stood by her side, looking hungrily at the defenseless, sleeping woman. Wilson licked his lips and reached out to place his hand on her cheek. "She looks mighty tempting, don't she? Been a long time since I had a woman this fine. Morgan sure knows how to pick 'em."

Paxton was out of his seat in an instant. Grabbing Wilson by the shoulder, he nearly threw the man across the room. "You get the hell away from her!" he shouted. Then turning to Kelly. "And don't you get any ideas in that walnut brain of yours either," he yelled.

Both Kelly and Wilson wondered what had come over their employer. Had he suddenly gone soft? He'd never denied them taking their pleasure wherever they found it before. Why was he now protecting this woman? Did he want her for himself? The two gunmen sat in the uncomfortable wooden parlor chairs, while Paxton returned to the plush chair from which he had been thinking.

Sensing that his men were waiting for an explanation for his strange behavior, Paxton began to reveal his plans. "I don't want this woman harmed in any way. We ain't got the upper hand any more," he admitted. "Folks in town are sure to be wondering why we rode in alone this morning, and if we start any trouble, they're apt to come after us. This woman is one of the town's upstanding citizens. She ain't some two dollar whore you boys can take any way you please. We're here for one reason and one reason only. And that's to use her to get Morgan. He's likely got his ranch back by now and is expecting us to come back for him. But that ain't how it's gonna be. Morgan's comin' in for us!

"But first we've gotta get this woman over to the jail without causing a scene. That means we're gonna have to sit around here till after dark. I just hope that that Chook character don't decide to up and run off. He's the one who has to deliver the message to Morgan."

"That'll get rid of him once and for all," Kelly said, chuckling. "Morgan'll kill him for sure."

Paxton looked at him sternly. "You're laughing now, but once Morgan gets the message, it's us he's gonna be out to kill. And don't you underestimate him, either. He's already got all but the three of us and once he hears that we've got his woman, he's gonna come after us with a vengeance. 'Cept he's likely as not to be half out of his mind with rage when he hears of it. He'll be even more dangerous then."

"What if the woman causes a fuss?" Wilson asked.

"Look at her." Paxton gestured with his hand. "Does this look like a woman who's gonna cause trouble?" Wilson laughed and then went into the kitchen to see what he could find to eat.

Sue had awakened a few moments before this while the men were still speaking. She had remained still and silent to hear what they were saying and what they had planned for her. She began trembling violently and finally opened her eyes when she could not control herself any longer.

Paxton saw her stirring but did not return to her side, thinking that she might faint again if she saw him again before fully regaining consciousness. Sue sat slowly on the couch, rubbing her eyes against the fog before her. When they finally cleared, she was aware of the sick feeling in her stomach.

"So, you've decided to join us," Paxton

said, loudly, to get her attention. "Not very hopsitable of you to fall asleep when guests arrive."

"You most certainly were not invited," Sue snapped, demonstrating some of the spirit that other women found so irritating.

Paxton shrugged off her remark. "I have not had the pleasure of seeing your Mr. Morgan since his return. How is he faring these days?"

Sue was about to make another cutting remark, but remembered Lee's warning about letting anyone know Morgan was back. "I wouldn't know. I had no idea Mr. Morgan was back." Sue tried to sound as cold as if she had never heard the man's name mentioned before. "I suppose that's why you're in town and not out pillaging his ranch." Sue caught herself before saying more. Her sharp tongue was going to get her in more trouble than she was already in if she wasn't careful.

"Well, Miz Clemons, you know as well as I that he has returned. But you may continue your little charade if you wish. It makes no difference to me." Paxton mocked her high-brow tone as he bit off the end of a fresh cigar. "I see you've been tidying up the house a bit. Could it be you *were* expecting company?"

"Unlike some others, I always keep myself clean. My house included. Why do you insist that I was expecting visitors?"

Paxton ignored her question. "In that case, you should work wonders over at the jail." He arched an eyebrow and waited for her response.

Sue would not give him the pleasure of seeming shocked. All she could think about was figuring out a way to get to the shotgun upstairs under her bed. Even if she could get one of them before they killed her, that would be one less man to go against Lee.

Sue and the two men sat quietly, Sue wondering just what kind of tortures they had planned for her. Wilson reentered with a tray of food, which he placed on the table in the middle of the room. "I see you've helped yourself," Sue said glumly.

Wilson returned to the chair with a sly smile spread across his face. "Not quite as much as I would have liked to," he said.

5

Chook had been pacing the floor of the old stone jailhouse nervously for almost three hours. He was beginning to feel more like a prisoner himself than a lawman. He hadn't been outside for more than five minutes since the afternoon of the day before. He'd tried reading a dime novel, playing solitare, even cleaning his firearms, but boredom and worry were getting the better of him. Where the hell was Paxton? At lunchtime he'd said he would be back within an hour or so. Now it was well after dark and there was still no sign of the man.

It had occured to Chook several times that maybe Paxton had had second thoughts about his plans for Morgan and had skipped town. Though that might have been the wisest choice for a man in Paxton's position, Chook didn't regard Paxton as a particularly rational man, especially after witnessing his burst of near-insane rage earlier that day.

At seven-o'clock, Chook couldn't stand it any longer. He had to find out for himself what had happened. He would first go over to Callaway's house to see if Paxton and his men had holed up there. After that he'd try the Black Ace. Someone in there must have seen them. Unless they stole a few horses, they must still be in town. Their own rides were still tied up outside, and getting very hungry.

Sam threw a couple of logs on the fire to keep the place warm while he was gone, then buckled on his holster and put on a light jacket, taking time to button it up to his neck. He left the light burning in his office and went to the front door, checking to make sure his gun was loaded. As an afterthought, Chook grabbed a shotgun on the way.

When he opened the front door, he was surprised to find a gun waving in his face. Without even seeing who was holding it, Chook knew it was Paxton.

"And where do you think you're going, Deputy?" Paxton demanded, pushing Chook back into the jailhouse with the barrel of the gun. "Get back in there and open this door as soon as I knock. I've got a little something out here I don't want to be seen."

Chook was too scared to respond, but closed the door again, leaving his hand on the knob so he could open it faster when Paxton returned.

Paxton went directly to the corner of the building and waved his men forward. They walked on either side of Suzanne Clemons, each leading her by an arm. Sue was dressed in her day dress, but was covered with a long flowing cape with an especially large hood that covered her face. If anyone were to see her going into the deputy's office, they would not have recognized her. As it was there was no one on the street, and Paxton was able to guide them inside without incident.

"Very good, Miz Clemons. You behaved exceedingly well out there," Paxton said as he pulled the cloak from Sue's head. Sue made her displeasure with the situation very evident. She drew back her hand to slap Paxton but stopped herself before striking him. There was no need to get him any more riled than he already was.

"Chook," Paxton said. "Please escort Miz Clemons to her new quarters, if you would. I'm sure you've tidied up the place for her."

Sue strutted through the front office to the cells at the end of the hall. For now she would cooperate—and pray that Lee was not foolish enough to fall into Paxton's trap.

She had not yet given any indication that she knew Morgan had returned, and if she could keep Paxton convinced that she was telling the truth, her demonstration of ignorance might work to her advantage. She might even make Paxton believe that she didn't care a whit for Lee Morgan.

As Chook shut the iron door and locked her in, Sue heard a knock at the front office door. Her heart sank. Surely Lee would not make such a direct approach . . . Then she heard Jesse Callaway's voice booming down the hallway.

"What's going on in here?" he demanded. "I thought you were going to get the girl. I've been watching from my office window for half the afternoon and ain't seen a blasted thing."

"Keep your damn voice down," Paxton said coldly. "The girl's locked up in the back. We had to wait till after dark to bring her in, else the whole town would know what we're up to."

Callaway lowered his voice a bit: "Well, you've certainly got 'em wondering. The town's been abuzz with rumors since you and your boys rode in this morning. Some say you're fixin' to pull out."

"I ain't pullin' out of nothin' till Morgan's dead and buried," Paxton spat.

"Like I told you this morning, I don't give a good goddam about that property out there. The whole place can burn to the ground again for all I care. I just want Morgan. And that pretty gal back there is gonna help me get him. I'd be willin' to bet that Morgan has his land back by now. But so what? Let him enjoy it for a few more hours. Come tomorrow, I'll have him planted out there forever."

"You ain't plannin' to hurt the Clemons girl, are you?" Callaway said, quietly. "Her father commands a lot of respect here in town. If folks hear that you've hurt her, you're apt to have more on your hands than you can handle."

"I ain't gonna harm a hair on her pretty little head, less she causes any trouble. Once Morgan's dead, she can go free and I'll never show my face around this two-bit town again."

She shivered, clasping her arms around herself as she sat on the cold, bare bench against the stone wall. What could Lee Morgan have possibly done to make this man hate him with such a passion? As long as she had known him, Lee had been a man who loved peace above all else. Yet he could never seem to find it. He had always lived as a hunted man—even after he had settled and decided to raise a family he was constantly on his guard.

The men's voices began dying down.

Sue resigned herself to doing what she could to make herself comfortable in the tiny cell. No one came to check on her so she blew out her lamp and crawled between the fresh sheets of the old cot fully dressed, not even bothering to remove her shoes. She lay there quietly trying to make out the men's voices but hearing only a lulling drone and the sound of bottles clanking.

She was nearly asleep when she was startled by the sound of several chairs scraping across the wooden floor. Sue guessed that she had been laying there half-awake for over two hours. That would make it after ten o'clock. It seemed that Paxton and his men hadn't drunk themselves into a stupor after all. She imagined they were preparing to leave. Callaway would of course go home. But Paxton had no place to go. Then she realized that he did. He and his men were going to her house, perhaps to sleep in her own bed. She was disgusted at the thought of it, but was powerless to keep them from her place. She prayed that it was all a dream, that tomorrow morning she would awaken in her own bed and start the day anew, with Paxton serving time in prison somewhere far away.

"Make sure you get plenty of rest," Paxton was saying to the deputy. "We'll be back before dawn tomorrow to rouse

you. Then you're headin' out to Spade Bit
to give Morgan our little message. If he
don't show his face in town by noon, his
little girl friend's body's gonna be strewn
along the trail from here to Boise. You
make sure he knows we mean business."

Paxton lumbered not quite drunkenly
out of the building, followed by his two
sharpshooters and Callaway, who looked
up and down the street before stepping
through the door.

Callaway was nervous, though he was
not quite as downhearted as he had been
earlier in the day, when Paxton had first
broken the news about Morgan winning
the ranch back. There was still a chance it
would be his, maybe before tomorrow was
over. As far as anyone knew, Morgan was
lying dead in the jungles of Panama. The
fact that the rumor was never proven
made some question Callaway's man-
euvering, especially Morgan's long-
time friends, like Sue Clemon's father, one
of the more vocal dissenters. Even if he
didn't see Morgan as a potential son-in-
law, he bought considerable amounts of
Morgan's horseflesh and didn't want that
business relationship disrupted.

Come tomorrow, Lee Morgan would be
forced to ride into town in full view of
everyone. And with Sue Clemons as
security, Morgan would surely be shot
dead in the street. Everyone would see it

happen, and Callaway would be free to take Spade Bit with no questions asked.

Jesse Callaway began to whistle a drunken tune as he walked toward the bank. He wanted to check the vault one last time before retiring to his home across town. The banker was so governed by money that he would have lived in the bank if there had been room. Then he would never have to leave the treasures that he considered his alone. Everything of value in town, from birth registrations to family heirlooms were locked in his vault. And that one little vault made him the most powerful man in Grover.

He wiped the sweat from his fat face with an already damp handkerchief as he climbed the wooden steps to the main level of the quiet, darkened building. He inserted the key, turned it in the lock and gingerly stepped inside, as if not to wake a sleeping baby. He walked straight to the vault and stopped before the mighty steel door. But instead of opening it to examine the fortune inside, he rubbed both of his hands over the smooth surface. Callaway dropped to his knees as if in prayer before some great icon. As he bowed his head, he began to feel tired—very tired—and in a moment sleep—an alcohol-induced sleep—overcame him, enveloping all thoughts of walking home.

This was his home.

* * *

With Paxton and his two goons gone, Deputy Chook returned to the bottle the men had not quite finished. He sat in one of the stiff wooden chairs and propped his feet on another. Without the use of a glass, he began to sip the whiskey slowly, wishing that it would steel him to the task that loomed before him, at the same time hoping that it might incapacitate him to the point that Paxton would have to send one of his own men.

But after a few sips, he resigned himself to going through with Paxton's scheme. At least he would be out of Paxton's reach for a time, and dealing with Morgan was a whole lot less deadly than working under Paxton's command. At least Morgan had a conscience.

His reputation in Grover as a lawman had been on the skids for some time, and his act of treachery against the town tomorrow would be enough to get him lynched if Morgan or Paxton didn't get him first. It was his lack of leadership and guts that had gotten him into this mess and he finally admitted to himself to be overwhelmed by men more powerful, mentally and physically, than himself, and there was nothing he could do to alter that now.

At length he stood up, thinking that he would turn in and let sleep dissipate his worries—at least for a few hours. He tossed the whiskey bottle into the wastebasket, then lined the chairs back up against the wall, taking time to make sure they were straight.

Chook struck a match and lit the small lamp that always sat on the table beside the front door. Then he blew out the rest of the lamps and headed for his stark room and the cold cot that awaited him. He couldn't help but think that this would be the last night he would spend there. Tomorrow night he would probably be buried under six feet of earth in potter's field, where all the criminals in town were buried.

He had just reached his room when he thought he would check up on Sue Clemons. As he approached her cell he held the lamp high to see into the interior. Sue was sleeping fitfully, still fully dressed. If Chook had not known her situation he would have thought she was sick with fever from the way she was tossing in her sleep. Her young face was damp with perspiration and contorted as though in pain.

He felt truly sorry for the woman. She had done nothing wrong. And if she had not had the misfortune to fall in love with Lee Morgan, she would have escaped this ordeal. Why did it have to be her? Why not Mary Spots? She, too, was a friend of

Morgan's. Yet as the most prominent whore in Grover, she would not be as sorely missed as Sue. In fact, there was a good many folks in Grover who would like to see her get her due.

But Paxton had chosen Sue for the most obvious reason. Lee Morgan was in love with her. Though Lee might not be able to admit this to himself, everyone who saw the two of them together knew this to be true, and Paxton had managed to pick up on this fact. Now Sue was a pawn in this feud just as much as Chook was. And she was apt to end up just as dead if things didn't go as Paxton wanted. In fact, it would be just like Paxton to kill her even after he had gotten his revenge on Morgan, just to prove that he could humiliate Morgan even in death.

Chook stood and stared at the woman for a full five minutes. What could he do to save her? After half a bottle of whiskey, he was no longer concerned for himself. As far as he was concerned, he was already dead. It didn't matter now if it was Morgan who killed him, or Paxton, or the territorial hangman. All that mattered to him now was seeing that Sue was kept safe.

Chook walked back to the front of the building and opened the front door. He left the front door open and stepped out onto the boardwalk. It seemed unusually dark outside. The moon had not yet risen and the stars twinkled dimly. A few gas street lamps were still lit, but no one walked the streets. A thin mist seemed to hang in the air, settling the dust from the main street. There was an eerie silence, the kind that occurs after a heavy snow.

So, Paxton had not had the forethought to post a guard. *He must be damn sure of himself,* Chook thought. For a moment the deputy considered taking his horse and riding out of town. But that would only delay his death for a few days at most. Paxton would surely hunt him down like a fox, and if that happened he might not die so swiftly. Out on the trail, Paxton could torture him for weeks if he desired.

Then he thought of Sue again. He could set her free: send her to her father's house until Paxton was gone. He owed Morgan at least that much. After all, Lee had not turned him in for his involvement in Callaway's last attempt to steal Spade Bit. Morgan could have had him put away for a long time, but chose not to. And, by all rights, Lee Morgan should have killed him the night before when he discovered Chook keeping guard over Sam and Luke. Still, he had let him go free. Morgan must have thought him still worth saving. For what, even Chook did not know. He had done nothing but betray Morgan's trust since they had first met. The least he could do would be to try to keep Sue from harm.

Chook went back inside the building, thankful for the warmth of the fireplace he had kept going. He immediately went to the small office that doubled as his bedroom. He placed the lamp on the night table and sat down on the edge of his cot. The shadow of his hunched form danced on the wall and made him seem almost animated. For long moments he sat there thinking and watching the flickering lamp. At length Chook slapped his knee and stood up. He would do it. He went directly to the little table where he kept the keys to the cell. His eyes bulged and opened wide as he pulled the drawer toward him. The keys! The keys were missing. He had always kept them there. And he was sure he had replaced them after he had locked up Sue Clemons.

So that was why Paxton had not bothered to post a guard outside. Paxton had stolen the only set of keys to the cell. No wonder he had been so trusting of Chook. He shut the drawer quickly, then opened it again, thinking that the set of keys might magically appear if he wished for it hard enough. But it was not to be. The keys were gone and there was no way he could let Sue out of her prison. Chook pounded his fist on the tabletop, startling even himself.

He was powerless. Paxton had outsmarted him and stolen not only the keys, but Chook's last chance to redeem himself. He stepped back, almost dazed. When he reached the cot, Chook sat down, lay back, then fell into a deep dreamless sleep.

Lee and Sam had spent the afternoon digging a pit in which to bury the seven lifeless bodies they had killed. By nightfall, with the hole finally covered, both men were exhausted and hungry.

Luke had proven himself to be stronger than either of them had expected. Despite his loss of blood, his body temperature rose steadily, and in the early evening he regained consciousness. Lee and Sam had been cleaning the house of the filth Paxton's men had brought in, and they took turns looking in on Luke. When Lee went in to throw a new log or two on the fire, Luke was laying on his side, trying to rise. Lee dropped the logs he was carrying and ran to the man.

"Lay back down there," he said gently but curtly enough to let Luke know that he meant business. Luke stared at Lee as if he barely recognized the man, but did as he was told.

"Where am I?" he asked quietly. "Last thing I remember I was behind a tree shooting at the window." Luke moved his hand over his bad arm until he flinched at the pain in his left shoulder. He looked at

Lee curiously. "I've been shot," he said.

"Rest easy," Lee said gently, encouraging the man to lay back on the mat in front of the hearth. "You keep these blankets on and that arm still, and you'll be all right. Paxton's men are dead and you're in the house. Sam and I have been tending your wounds since this afternoon. You lost a lot of blood, so you're gonna stay right where you are until you get your senses back." Lee turned away from the man for a moment. "Sam," he called downstairs. "Bring up a big bowl of that vegetable soup you made. We have a patient up here that needs some nourishment."

"Paxton's men . . . dead?" Luke was asking through a grimace.

"We got all the ones here in the house, thanks to you and Sam. We've got the ranch back—for now. But I'd be willing to bet that Paxton and his other two goons are still in town. Ain't much I can do about that as long as you're laid up. We'll just have to wait and see what happens."

Lee turned his face to look at Luke, and realized that Luke had drifted off to sleep again. While the man was unconscious, Lee changed his dressing, all the time hoping—praying—that Luke would recover well enough to shoot again before Paxton returned with his reinforcements.

After throwing the logs into the dying

fire, Lee went down to the kitchen. "Cancel that order," he said to Sam, who was busy reheating soup over the stove.

"Is-is he all right?" Sam asked, fearing Lee meant that Luke was dead.

"He'll be okay—in time," Lee reassured him. "He woke up for a few minutes—just long enough to find out where he was. I thought he might eat something, but he was still too delirious to stay awake. Maybe he'll come around tomorrow."

It was just before dawn when Lee Morgan dragged himself out of bed. He pulled on his trousers, buckled on his gunbelt, then opened the windowshade. The air was fresh and cold from the night, but the aura of death from the day before still lingered.

It seemed so peaceful outdoors, and he recalled why he so loved sleeping under the stars. Though all the rooms of the house were built especially spaciously, Lee could not help but feel closed in, restrained from living the way God had meant for man to live. He suddenly found himself questioning his resolve to keep Spade Bit. Everything about it was confining. Owning the place was a hindrance in many ways, the most significant of which was that he could not leave it unattended. He had to be there constantly to protect his property, his horses, the men he hired; and now he was being drawn to what might be another disastrous marriage—all because he had given up the life of a drifter. And for what purpose? Because he was tired? For the sake of his dead father?

It really didn't matter. What was done was done. He wasn't about to revert to his old ways. People respected him now, and that was something he had never had as a gunman. People used to fear him. But respect was something that was even harder to come by. And he was grateful for it.

Downstairs, he got the coffee going, and after it had been perking for a few minutes he heard Sam stirring and shuffling around in the upstairs bedroom.

"Mr. Morgan," Sam called out. "Can you come up here?"

"Be right there," Lee shouted back. He wrapped a linen towel around the handle of the coffee pot and grabbed a couple of cups. With his hands full, he bounded up the stairs toward the bedroom. "What's the matter?" Lee asked before he even entered the room. It suddenly occurred to him that Paxton and his men might be launching an early attack. "We got company?"

"In a manner of speaking," Sam said as Lee passed through the door frame. Lee saw the smirk on Sam's face and was just about to cuss him out for playing games, when, out of the corner of his eye, he saw Luke. He was sitting upright on the bed, his eyes clear and alert.

A big grin of relief spread over Lee's face, as much for his own sake as for Luke's. "Well, well. Welcome back among the livin' and breathin'. How you feelin', pardner?"

"Like a freight train just ran over my arm. How about pourin' some of that coffee and gettin' me a bite to eat. I'm famished."

"Look at him," Lee said to Sam in mock seriousness. "He gets a pampering and a good night's sleep and now he's givin' orders like he owns the place."

"If you don't get me healthy enough to handle a gun again, Callaway's the one likely be owning this place." Though the remark was meant as a joke, Lee knew that Luke was right on that point.

Lee tried to keep the tone from becoming too serious. "Okay, tough guy. Breakfast coming up. And take it easy on that coffee until you get something solid in your belly."

Lee returned to the kitchen and the search for edible food. The previous tenants had left sparse provisions. It seemed that, having failed in their attempts to cook on a stove, they had left the burned pans and charred food to rot, eating only what they did not have to cook.

Lee found a few still-fresh eggs, and a big slab of salt-cured ham that had somehow been overlooked. There was flour but no milk and not enough eggs to make flapjacks. Sighing, he set to work making do with what he had. Sam had done a good job the night before of cleaning out the kitchen, but Lee still wished his housekeeper was around to do this chore. Better yet, he wished he were sitting in Sue Clemon's fine dining room, waiting to be served one of her delicious southern-style meals.

The voice came from upstairs. "Mr. Morgan, I think you better get up here again, and be quick about it." Lee moved the skillet full of solidifying eggs away from the stove and ran up the stairs two at a time. This time there was no smile on Sam's face as Lee entered the room. He had a gun drawn and was standing to the side of one of the room's tall windows.

"Paxton?" Lee managed to spit out as he duck-walked his way to the window beside Sam.

"Too far away yet to tell," Sam said. "But I don't think so. It's just one rider, and Paxton ain't got the guts to ride out here alone."

"That's no lie," Lee said, watching the dust being kicked up half a mile away. "Whoever it is looks like he's in a God-awful hurry. Better load up the rifles just in case there's more of 'em comin' up behind him."

Sam crouched down and crossed the room to where Luke was sitting. There, he loaded the three rifles, tossed one over to Lee, and handed another to Luke, who was struggling to get out of the bed.

"Stay in the bed," Sam said. "There's only one rider out there. If there's any more, you'll get your chance."

Luke stopped struggling, despite wanting to see what was going on. He leaned back against the mahogany headboard and let the rifle lay across his lap, pointed in the general direction of the bedroom door.

As the mounted man drew closer, Lee could see that the horse he rode was not one of his own. Despite the speed with which the rider came, the horse seemed uneasy, as if on unfamiliar ground. It was a horse that had not seen too many days out on the open trail.

As the rider neared the ranch house, he began to slow the horse to a walk. For a moment he even stopped and began to fumble for something in one of the saddlebags. Lee and Sam watched intently as the man unfolded a white handkerchief and held it aloft as he began to ride in again.

"Well, whoever it is, he's smart enough

to know that he's not apt to be welcome here." Lee gave out his instructions. "You stay up here and keep him covered from the window. I'm going down to see what this is all about. If there's any trouble at all, you just pull that trigger." Lee walked to the door. "And holler if you spot any more riders!" he added, as if coaching a child.

Lee's spurs clanked on the stairs as he went down. This was no neighborly visit from a farmer, and it sure wasn't Paxton. Everyone in town knew about the trouble out at Spade Bit. Why would someone venture out here?

He stepped out into the soft morning sunlight and walked to the middle of the lawn. Leaves were blown about his feet, and the cool air left his cheeks slightly numb. Lee stood with his legs apart, his arms crossed as if in defiance, and waited for the man to come nearer.

The man wore an oilskin overcoat, making him seem bigger than he actually was. Lee did not recognize the horse, but when the morning breeze blew open the coat, he did recognize the badge.

"Chook," he said aloud to himself. "What the devil is he doing out here?" He had to have started well before dawn to get here this early. Lee's look of determination changed to amusement as the sad looking man approached him.

Paxton must have put some scare into him back in Grover.

The deputy looked at Lee Morgan solemnly, then dismounted slowly. He blew his runny nose on the white handkerchief he had been waving, then tucked it into his trouser pocket.

"What's this all about, Deputy?" Lee asked the man, when it looked like Chook was going to have a hard time spitting out what he wanted to say. Water began to well up in Chook's eyes.

"Paxton sent me out here," Chook said, wiping his nose on his sleeve. "And considering the circumstances, I thought I'd better do as he wants."

"And just what are those circumstances?" Lee asked, ignoring the man's emotion. "Paxton threaten to skin you alive if you didn't?"

"That ain't it!" Chook said determinedly. "I don't care anymore what he does to me. Anything I do's gonna get me killed, so I may as well try to do something right for a change. Who knows, maybe the good Lord will have a little pity on me."

Lee began to turn angry. "Quit your babbling and sniveling and get to the point. You didn't ride out here for nothing. Spit it out, man!"

"I came out here to tell you what Paxton was planning . . ." Chook looked down at his dusty boots, and then back at Morgan.

"Well?" Morgan pressed. "Let's hear it."

"I think maybe you better be sittin' down when I tell you this. Can we go inside the house?"

"Anything you got to tell me, you can say right here and right now. Now speak up, or I'll shoot you where I stand." Lee was fuming now. "What's Paxton got on his mind? When's he ridin' in here and how many men has he got with him?"

Deputy Chook took off his hat and held it over his chest. "That's just it, Mr. Morgan. Paxton ain't planning to ride back in here. It ain't your ranch he wants, it's you. He wants you in town before noon today."

"He wants me in town before noon today," Lee repeated, almost laughing at the idea. "Did you hear that, Sam?" Lee hollered toward the upstairs window. "Paxton wants me to come in after him." Still laughing, Lee turned back to face Chook. "And just what makes him think I'm willing to oblige him?"

Chook looked toward the heavens for a moment, as if saying his final prayers, then he met Morgan's gaze with near-lifeless eyes. "Cause if you don't show, he's gonna murder Suzanne Clemons!"

The words stung Lee Morgan as if he had been slapped. He was too dazed to even respond. "Murder Sue Clemons!" Those words echoed endlessly through his head, contorting and twisting all reasoning into a violent ball of rage.

How could this happen? He had given her explicit instructions not to give any indication that she knew he had returned. Yet the worst had happened. Paxton had discovered Morgan's soft spot, and now he was as vulnerable as a newborn's skull.

He wanted to take Chook's head in his hands and twist it until the neck snapped. But Lee still had enough sense to know that this was not the deputy's fault. As much as Lee wanted to kill right then, Chook was not the man he wanted. He had to get at the man, who for the second time, was getting at him through the woman he loved. And this he would not stand for.

Chook stood shivering before him, waiting for the death blow that was sure to come. He closed his eyes and clutched his hat even closer to him. But there was no blow, nor a shot from one of Lee Morgan's infamous Colts. When he opened his eyes again, Lee was gone, as if he had never been standing there, as if none of this had really happened.

Lee was on the stoop of the year-old porch with his rifle slung over his shoulder, staring at the shell of a man in the middle of his yard. If he put a bullet through him right now, he might be doing them both a favor. Paxton would no longer have a lackey to be his gopher, and Chook would no longer be tormented by the man who had shattered his spirit. He slung the rifle to his shoulder and took aim at just the same time he came into Chook's field of vision.

His finger touched the trigger gently, testing it as if to see just how much pressure it would take before igniting the charge and sending the slug into Chook's chest. At the other end of the barrel stood Chook, passively, waiting for the inevitable.

For the first time in his life, Lee Morgan had aimed a gun at a man he intended to kill, but could not pull the trigger. It would be like shooting a puppy for misbehaving. Still, he did not lower the weapon. Chook looked at him blankly, wondering again why he was not dead.

"I ought to do it," Lee said simply.

"I didn't expect that you wouldn't," Chook responded. "I knew you'd probably kill me on the spot, but even if Paxton hadn't planned for me to come out here, I would've anyway. For your sake and for Sue Clemons."

Chook was still a weasel, but Morgan felt genuinely touched by the man's admission. Maybe there was some hope left for him after all.

Lee lowered the barrel of his rifle until it was pointed at the ground just in front of

Chook's feet. "Drop your sidearm on the ground in front of you," Lee said.

Chook did as he was asked. Could it be true that Morgan wasn't going to kill him after all?

"Now that Winchester," Lee went on. "Take it out of the holster and put it on the ground by the gun . . . and don't throw it!" Again Chook complied with what Lee said.

"Now take your horse to the barn with the others, then get your ass into the house."

Chook did not waste any time making for the barn. When he returned, his firearms were no longer laying on the front lawn and Lee Morgan had disappeared into the house. Chook stepped up to the porch and knocked on the door.

"Stop wastin' time and get in here," Morgan shouted from somewhere within. Chook pushed the door open and adjusted his eyes to the dimmer light. There was a rustling in the kitchen and Chook went to investigate. As soon as he stepped in, Lee stuck a fork in his hand and pointed him to the stove. "Make yourself useful and turn that ham. On accounta you, breakfast is getting cold."

Chook was awed by Morgan's nonchalance and seeming lack of concern for the safety of Sue Clemons. Maybe he didn't care for her as much as Paxton had suspected. Perhaps the time he had spent in Panama had distanced him from her. Neither of them passed a word as they worked in the kitchen and when Lee headed upstairs with the completed breakfast, Chook followed like an obedient sheep.

Sam was at the window, keeping a lookout over the trail leading directly from town. "You might as well sit down and have a bite," Lee said to him. "There ain't nobody else coming, least not Paxton, noways. Looks like I'm gonna have to go in after him."

Luke and Sam looked at him as if to ask, "Why bother?" Lee served everyone a helping of ham and eggs and handed the coffee pot to Chook, who poured a cup and sipped it black.

Luke ventured a first question. "What the hell's this crooked deputy doing here? That's the same jackass that had me locked up." Luke made as if to rise, then gripped his shoulder in pain. "Damn!" he said. "If I warn't so busted up, I'd kick his tail all the way to the marshal's office in Boise." Luke took an oversized bite of ham and leaned back to chew, all the while glaring at the deputy.

Chook sat quietly sipping coffee and taking small bites of food white Sam and Luke grumbled over his presence. Though Chook had resigned himself to dying, he was thankful that Lee Morgan was at least being civil to him. Considering what he had done, each man present had every reason to want to beat the man to a pulp.

"Keep your thoughts to yourself, Luke," Lee was saying. "The deputy here ain't done right by us, but I didn't hear tell of you standing up to Paxton when he rode into Spade Bit, either. Chook might not be the most honest deputy in Idaho, but everything he's done has been at the point of Paxton's gun. He ain't innocent, but he ain't as guilty as he might be either." Lee sopped the rest of his runny eggs with a hunk of ham and popped the morsel into his mouth. Then he washed the whole thing down with a gulp of cooling coffee.

"It looks like Chook here's had a change of heart about who's side he's on," Lee continued, casting a sidelong glance in the deputy's direction. "He's rode all the way out here this morning to tell me what Paxton's up to. And believe me, it don't look good." He paused for another sip.

Chook looked at Morgan curiously, wondering why Lee was lying for him, why Lee did not tell them that he had actually come out on orders from Paxton. He was certain that Morgan was developing some sort of scheme to rescue Sue, and judging from Morgan's behavior, he guessed that it involved him. Had Morgan spared his life just to send him into the jaws of the lion?

"Well . . . ?" Sam urged Lee for an elaboration.

"I don't have the full story yet," Lee said, "but it seems that Paxton is getting desperate. He and the two men he has left are planning to kill Sue Clemons if I haven't shown my face in town by noon today."

Sam jumped to his feet, nearly knocking over his plate. "Miss Clemons!" he shouted in astonishment. "He's gonna kill her?"

"Looks that way," Lee said, with an unusual calmness.

"How can you just sit there and eat breakfast when she's gonna be dead in a couple of hours? We've gotta get in there and . . ."

"Sit down Sam!" Lee said, becoming irritated with Sam's outburst. "It ain't even seven yet. That gives me more than five hours. It don't take but an hour to get into Grover. The first thing we gotta do is hear out the deputy here. He's gonna tell us everything that's going on in town, aren't you, Deputy?"

All eyes were on Chook now, each man waiting for the full story, and each wondering if he would tell the truth, or concoct some lie to further ingratiate himself with Paxton.

"There ain't much more to tell than I've already told you, Lee. Paxton rode in yesterday morning snapping like a mad dog 'cause you'd killed off his best men. And he wasn't about to turn tail and run. He went over to talk to Callaway about something which he never told me. He made me stay in the jailhouse all day while he went over and kidnapped the Clemons girl."

Lee cut in: "Why didn't you come out here to tell me while he was out all day?"

"I figured if he knew I had gone to warn you last night, he would have killed her on the spot, just out of spite."

"I see," Lee said. "Well, go on."

"Anyway, he come back about seven last night with the girl all wrapped up in a cape. She didn't put up no fight neither. Came in real quiet-like. Paxton made me lock her up in one of the cells and I guess she went right off to sleep. Least we didn't hear a peep out of her anyways. After that, Paxton and the boys kicked back in the office and started celebratin' with a bottle of whiskey. They damn near finished the whole bottle, too.

"Oh, I forgot to mention that Jesse Callaway stopped in, too. Guess Paxton must have told him earlier to meet them in the office. Anyway, they all got pretty drunk toasting victory over and over again. Finally Callaway said he had to get home. Paxton and his boys cleared out too. I think they were going over to Miss Clemons' house for the night.

"After they were gone, I was fixin' to let her out and send her over to her daddy's house to hide out, but that son-of-a-bitch Paxton swiped my only set of keys. There warn't nothing I could do then. I must have passed out on my cot, 'cause the next thing I knew, Paxton was shaking me awake. That was a couple of hours ago. Within a half hour, I was on my way out here to tell you what he wanted."

Chook was honestly shaken now. He bent his head low and grasped at his thin, sandy hair with both hands. When he looked up again, his eyes were red. "If only I coulda gotten her out. Paxton woulda killed me and then probably left town without you. Then none of this would be happening."

"Was she hurt?" Lee asked. "If they touched . . ."

Chook cut Lee off before his imagination ran away with him. "She wasn't hurt as of this morning, or at least she didn't complain of it if she was. I don't doubt that those boys of Paxton's would like to do a few ungentlemanly things to her. But I don't think Paxton would let them. He ain't got no fight with the lady, Lee, and he don't intend to hurt her unless you don't show up this morning. But if it meant the difference between getting back at you and running with his tail between his legs again, I don't doubt that he'd kill her in an instant. The man's gone half mad since he got wind that you were back. He's apt to do just about anything to see you die."

Chook was quiet now, along with everyone else in the room, and the only sound came from the popping of the green logs in the fireplace. Lee had been expecting a straight fight to the finish between him and however many men Paxton could rustle up, and he had planned to spend the morning making preparations for defense around the ranch house, but Paxton's new tactic changed everything. Now he was dragging innocents into the fight as well.

"Well . . ." Sam said at length. "Are we going in or are we gonna sit here all day? Sue Clemons' life is at stake."

Lee noticed that a change had come over Sam. He seemed much bolder now than he had when Lee had first returned. Then Lee realized what it was. One day he was just a naive cowpoke trying to collect enough wages to live on, the next day he's thrown into prison, forced into a gunfight, and faced with rescuing a female prisoner —enough action to make a man out of anybody.

"*We're* not gonna do anything," Lee said. "It's me Paxton's after and it's me he's gonna get. Luke, you're too weak to be walking around, much less holding a gun. And somebody's got to stay here to look after him. That's you, Sam!"

"What!" Sam gasped. "Are you crazy? You're not thinking of riding in there alone?"

Lee smiled at the young man's enthusiasm. "No, I'm not. Deputy Chook is going to accompany me."

No one was more stunned by this than Chook himself. He would rather that Morgan had shot him dead on the lawn than return to Grover to face Paxton again. That would truly be a fate worse than death.

"You can't possibly mean that," Sam raged on. "That man is in cahoots with Paxton and Callaway. He'll probably kill you as soon as your back is turned."

"I don't intend to turn my back," Lee said. "But I'm willing to bet that he won't do it." Lee shot Chook a look that said that he'd better agree. Chook nodded in assent.

"Then at least take us with you," Sam said.

"I want you here," Lee insisted. "The two of you have done enough fighting for me. This last battle is my own. Besides, I can get into town unnoticed by myself. If we all come charging in together, we're likely to put a scare into Paxton and get Sue killed. You two stay. Agreed?"

Sam and Luke nodded, then turned their heads away from him, unable to look him in the eyes.

"Shall we ride, Deputy?" asked Lee, standing.

"Guess so," Chook said and eased himself to his feet. "Hope you know what you're doing," he mumbled, thinking that Lee had not heard.

"So do I," said Lee. "For both our sakes, so do I."

6

Lee had insisted that Chook leave the horse he had ridden in on and take one of Morgan's finest instead, the same one Luke had ridden the day before. Chook had his arms back, and though he had no intention of shooting Morgan, he wondered that Lee trusted him enough to give them back. Morgan even took the lead position on the trail giving Chook a clear shot at his back.

Lee was traveling light. He had stripped the horse of all gear except the saddle, a canteen, and the rifle, which he kept in its holster, but readily available.

Both mounts were fresh and stepped lively as they picked their way over the rocky trail. The sun was still low in the sky, and there was less than an hour of easy riding ahead of them. Lee calculated that they would reach Grover well before nine—plenty of time to scout out the situation. Once out of the trees and riding up the slope that led to the main road, Chook stepped his horse up alongside Morgan's.

After they had ridden in this fashion for a few moments, Chook ventured to speak. "Morgan, I still don't know why you didn't kill me back there when you had the chance. Just what kind of help are you expecting to get from me?"

Lee tipped his hat back but did not look Chook's way. "Deputy, I have the chance to kill you any time I want. Be thankful that you've got the chance to clear yourself in front of everyone in Grover. You won't get another. As for what I expect out of you, the answer is nothing. You can turn tail and run back to Paxton as soon as we get to town if you want, but all you're gonna get from him is a bullet, when all this is done. It's your choice."

Lee did not see the man nod, but knew that Chook would get his meaning. It was likely that they would both die today, and Lee was giving him one last chance to come out clean. If Chook could gather up the guts to stand with Morgan against Paxton, all of his past infractions would be overlooked by the townsfolk.

Chook tried Lee's patience with another question. "Have you got any kind of plan?

I mean, you can't just walk in there and call him out. He'd just haul Miss Clemons out and hold a gun to her head till his boys gunned you down. Where would that get you?"

"It wouldn't get me nowhere." Lee said without emotion. "That's why I ain't gonna do it."

"Well, what then?" Chook urged.

"Guess I'll have to think of something before we get there, won't I? 'Sides, I've got a couple of stops to make before we get down to business at hand." Chook started to drop back to a position behind Lee again, but Lee waved him back alongside him. He reached into his jacket pocket and pulled out one of the three sticks of dynamite he had the forethought to bring. Chook's eyes widened when he saw it, and nearly popped out of their sockets when Lee tossed it over to him without pause.

"Stick that in your inside jacket pocket and don't forget it's there," Lee said. Then he reached inside his shirt pocket and pulled out a pair of cigars he had picked up in New Orleans. One he stuck in his own mouth and the other he thrust toward Chook. "Have a cigar," he said.

Chook looked at it and then at Lee, wondering what was going on. "No thanks," he said. "I don't smo—"

"Start," Lee said sharply, placing the

end of the stogie into Chook's open mouth.

After that, Chook shut up, puzzled by Morgan's actions. By the time they reached the main road a mile outside Grover, Luke and Sam were already conspiring to saddle up and follow them.

It was still early enough that Lee did not have to worry about being seen by anyone on the road, and even if they did pass someone, they would be riding out of town. At the first sign of activity up ahead, however, the pair pulled off the road and headed north through the sparse trees. Despite the influx of new settlers in recent years, it was still beautiful country. Country worthy fighting and dying for, Lee reminded himself.

"Where we headed?" Chook said in an unnaturally loud whisper.

"Friend of mine's house," Lee replied. "Someone who's got just as much at stake in this as I do."

"Reckon he'll help you out?" Chook asked.

"If this man don't, he ain't fit to live," Lee answered.

They rode together for another half mile, leaves crunching under their feet, the wind in their faces. By the time they reached the little cabin just to the north of town, Chook's thin skin was nearly numb.

"That's the place," Lee said, pointing

with his arm.

Before them was a tidy little cabin with a well-attended yard. Smoke billowed from the tall stone fireplace and a fresh coat of whitewash covered the planking of the walls. Lee and Chook followed a chopping sound to the north side of the house, where wood was piled as high as the windows and a tall, lean man in his fifties was hard at work chopping more.

As the two riders came into view, the man stopped splitting wood and looked up to see who his visitors were.

"Well, I'll be! Lee Morgan, back in Grover. I'd all but given you up for dead. When did you get back?"

"Just yesterday," Lee said. He got off his mount and stretched a hand out to the man, who took it gratefully. "I been out at the ranch taking care of some business."

"Oh, yeah. I been hearing stories that there was trouble brewing out there while you were away. Hope you got it all staightened out."

"Not quite," Lee said. "Chook, get down here."

The man looked at Chook as if for the first time and asked, "What are you doing riding with the deputy, Lee? I ain't got no trouble out here. Been cuttin' a supply of timber all morning."

"Don't think I've had the pleasure, sir," Chook cut in, offering his hand and a friendly smile. The man took it and returned a nervous grin.

"Deputy, this here is Jim Clemons, Suzanne's father." Lee spoke the words as much in warning as in introduction.

The smile immediately disappeared from Chook's face and he released the grip he had on the man's hand. "Pleased to meet you," he managed to say.

Jim Clemons was more than curious now. "Lee, what's going on here? I know you didn't ride all the way out here to introduce me to the deputy. You in some kind of trouble?"

"Jim," Lee said with caution, "I think we'll need to go inside to discuss this with you."

Within fifteen minutes the house was empty again and the three men were on their way along the path from which Morgan and Chook had come. Lee led the way as they crossed the main road and into the woods on the other side, Jim cursing every step of the way, spouting in graphic detail just what he intended to do to Paxton.

"We've got one more stop to make," Lee said to the men when they were well into the woods. As they made the wide circle to the other side of the town, Chook kept looking at his pocket watch. The morning was wearing on, and still Morgan hadn't indicated what he was planning. When they finally broke the trees, the trio walked their horses along the back of the buildings facing Main Street, ignoring the stares from the people they passed.

They stopped in back of the bank building and dismounted. It wasn't an imposing structure, no bigger than most of the other stores around it, but then Grover wasn't an imposing town. Still, it was the sturdiest building in town and one of the oldest. Word had it that Jessie Callaway spent more time there than he did at home.

"Chook, I want you to stay here and mind the horses," Lee said. "Jim and I have a little business to take care of inside."

"What the hell are you wasting time for, Morgan," Chook protested. "The bank ain't even open yet, anyway."

"It ain't open for regular business," Lee said in a condescending tone, as if explaining a simple math problem to a child. "But I know Callaway comes in early to make sure all his pennies are in place, and the business I got with him ought not be done around customers."

Lee and Clemons handed Chook the reins of their horses and disappeared into the alley that led to the front of the building. The street was swarming with people, though all were too busy with their own affairs to even notice Lee and his companion mounting the bank steps. When they reached the top, Lee pounded on the door and was amazed to see it swing open at his touch.

Lee and Jim looked at one another in query. "Something ain't right here," Lee observed. "It ain't like Callaway to leave the door open before banking hours, even if he is in."

Lee pushed the door open even wider and peered inside the dark open room. There didn't seem to be anyone moving about as Lee stepped inside with Clemons close behind. A dim light filtered in through the high windows, illuminating the heavy dust in the air, and casting eerie patterns on the floor. Jim closed the door behind him, making it even harder to see.

It was Clemons who saw him first. Callaway, sprawled like a limp bag of rags by the vault door. The mystery here was becoming deeper with every passing moment.

Both men rushed to his side. Jim grabbed his wrist to check the pulse, but Lee could spell the whiskey and had already guessed what the trouble was.

"He don't seem to be hurt," Jim said.

"Course he don't," Lee said. "The fool's dead drunk." Lee bent down and took Callaway's keys from the end of the chain attached to his belt. He tossed them to

Jim, who cast Morgan a curious look. "Well, don't just stand there. Open the vault."

Jim stared at the keys in his hand. "I don't know about this," he said. "I came with you to get my daughter back, not rob no bank."

"Who said anything about robbing the bank," Lee said, bending down and slapping Callaway across the face repeatedly. "Just open the door."

Clemons tried two keys before finding the one that fit the huge door. As it turned in the lock, the door eased open quietly on well-oiled hinges. Callaway was regaining his senses, though Lee had to shake him to bring him fully awake.

"What—what is it you want? What is this?" Callaway stuttered, his eyelids fluttering, his speech still slurred and nearly incoherent.

"Get up!" Lee snapped.

Callaway's eyes suddenly focussed on the source of the voice that had so abruptly awakened him. "Lee Morgan! What the hell . . . Where did you come from? Where the hell am I?"

"Get on your feet, you drunken fool. You're in your own damn bank," Lee said.

Callaway struggled to his feet and looked around him, then began brushing off his clothes, trying to look as dignified as possible considering his predicament.

"How did you get in here?" he demanded, putting on airs.

"Just walked in the front door you left unlocked," Lee said, shoving Callaway toward the vault.

Callaway's eyes widened when he saw Clemons standing next to the open vault door, twirling the key ring on his forefinger. "What're you doing with my keys? You can't go in there." Callaway was vainly attempting to play innocent. "Who's that man?" he snapped, though he knew exactly who he was and why he was there.

Lee didn't answer but led Callaway by the arm to the inside of the vault. "Damn it, Morgan! I can't believe you'd stoop so low as to rob the same bank where you keep your money." The inside of the vault was dry and dark and uncommonly quiet, forbidding enough, but it was far from airtight: the perfect place to put Callaway for safekeeping.

"Make yourself comfortable," Lee said. "We'll be back for you just as soon as the Marshal gets here from Boise."

Callaway hung his head, knowing that his time had come. But then the life came back into his eyes when he realized what Lee meant. "But that's forty miles from here," he said. "I'll be in here all day!"

"And all night," Lee continued. "You

see, no one's gone up to get him yet."

Lee pulled the heavy door shut and Jim Clemons turned the key again. "Not a bad little trick," he said to Lee, slapping him on the back. "Shall we try for Mr. Paxton now?"

"It will be a pleasure," Lee said, taking the keys and putting them in his jacket pocket. Inside the vault, Callaway's frantic screams could almost be heard.

At the back of the building, Chook was still standing with the horses when Lee and Jim returned. Deciding it was best to do without them, they unfastened their rifles and checked the loads. Then Lee sat down on an old water bucket and explained what they would do.

Five minutes later Lee and Jim were on their way to Sue Clemons' house on Main Street. Chook was making his way to the jailhouse and his final confrontation with Billy Paxton.

The jailhouse door was locked when Chook arrived, but when he reached for his keys, he realized that Paxton still had them. He pounded on the door loud enough to wake anyone inside. Seconds later Paxton opened it, and Chook found himself staring down the barrel of Paxton's gun. He swallowed once hard, and Paxton pulled him into the building by his lapel.

"Where is he?" Paxton demanded.

"I told him you was at Sue Clemons' place, just like you said," Chook answered, not quite as frightened as he had been with Paxton in the past. "He's headed over there aimin' to gun you down all by himself. Soon as he took off, I ran over here to tell you." Chook skirted telling Paxton about the presence of Sue's father.

Paxton got a big, evil looking grin on his face. "Everything's coming together just as I planned," he said. He called to his men sitting at the table playing cards. Sue Clemons was there, too, and Chook wondered why Paxton had let her out of the cell. "Get up, you lazy sons-of-bitches. Morgan's over at the girl's house just waiting for you to come over and pick him off. Get over there and don't come back until he's dead." The two men got up and walked out the front door as if they were going to church.

"This is going to be easier than I thought," Paxton said aloud. "And even if they don't finish him off, I've still got you, Miz Clemons. You'll draw him over here like a moth to a light." He took her by the arm and threw the cell keys to Deputy Chook. "Deputy, take her in the back and lock her up. I don't want her up here gabbing and carrying on like a baby. Wilson and Kelly'll be back soon and we're getting out of town, just as soon as we collect a small fee from Callaway for getting Morgan out of the way."

Chook nodded and jingled the keys. Sue frowned at the deputy but preceeded him to the cell where she had spent the night. "You call yourself a lawman," she whispered to him on the way back. "You ought to be ashamed of yourself."

Once in her cell, Sue returned to her bunk and glared at the deputy, who was nervously fumbling with the keys. He pulled the cell door to, then fastened the keys to his belt without locking it. Then he cast a look toward the main office to see if Paxton was checking up on him. He was not. "I'm leaving the door open,' Chook whispered to Sue, who couldn't believe her ears. "If you see a chance to get out of here, take it. You won't get another." Then he turned to rejoin Paxton before she had the chance to ask questions.

"Now, it's your turn," Paxton said. "Give me those keys."

"What do you mean?" Chook asked, becoming nervous once again. Getting locked up was one thing he had not counted on. "Why are you locking me in the cell? I did what you asked."

"You'll get out," Paxton said. "The minute Morgan is dead." They walked back down the hallway to the cell next to Sue's and Chook gave her a little nod just before Paxton shoved him into the little room.

Sue understood that this was her only chance. While Paxton was concentrating on locking Chook's door, Sue grabbed the lamp next to her bed and returned to the door. Paxton hadn't even realized that she was there and would not have expected her to do what she did even if he had known. Without a word, Sue stuck her hand through the bars and hit Paxton squarely on the head with the lamp, sending shattered glass and oil spraying all over the hall and into Chook's cell. Paxton collapsed in a heap on the floor.

Sue was almost afraid to come out of her cell, for fear that something else dreadful would happen. Paxton was conscious, but barely. He rolled on the floor holding his head and moaning.

"Miss Clemons, are you there?" Chook called.

"Yes," she said, still unable to comprehend what she had just done.

"Well, what are you standing there for? Run and get help. Paxton's liable to come to any minute, and if you're here when he does, I wouldn't want to be here to see what he does to you."

Sue came out of the cell. "But what about you?" she said scanning the floor for the keys but unable to find them. "I can't just leave you here."

"Don't worry about me," Chook implored. "Just get out of here. Go get your father and Morgan. They're both at your house."

Sue didn't understand what was going on, but she did as Chook asked and ran from the building, leaving Paxton rolling on the floor in pain and the deputy there to face the consequences when he recovered. She would have to get to Lee fast.

Lee and Jim had a little surprise waiting for Wilson and Kelly when the latter two arrived at Sue's house. While Jim waited for the attack from inside the house, Lee stood across the street where he would have a commanding view of the approach to the house. Within twenty minutes, Paxton's men came lumbering down the street toward Sue's house. Both were walking as though nothing were amiss, though when they neared the house, both ducked into the alleyway and headed for the back, looking furtively for anyone that might have seen them. Lee went into action. He ran to the front door and knocked three times to alert Jim, then he drew his Colts and hugged the wall to the back of the building.

Inside, Jim made ready. He ducked behind the couch and aimed his Winchester toward the back window. There was a crash and in an instant both Wilson and Kelly were in the parlor with their guns drawn. Clemons ducked, not expecting such an abrupt entry. His sudden movement caught Wilson's eye.

"There he is, behind the couch," Wilson shouted. And both men began pumping bullets into it. Though he was laying on the floor, Clemons felt a slug tear through his leg and yelled out in pain. Now he was totally helpless. Paxton's men had him just where they wanted him—flat on the floor and unable to return fire. And when the found out he wasn't Morgan, they would have no mercy. But where was Morgan?

Kelly and Wilson had each finished the rounds in one gun and were just drawing out their other six-shooters to move in for the kill. They only had time to see Morgan's shadow stretching out on the floor before they realized that they had been set up. Both men spun around to see Lee Morgan standing in the doorway with both Colts drawn. He shot Wilson in the face before the man had even registered recognition. Wilson tore at his blood-soaked face as if trying to hold himself together, but he was dead even before he crumpled to the floor. Kelly got off one shot which flew by Morgan's head and out the door, before Morgan shot him in the stomach, sending him flying across the room and into the couch. He looked at Morgan with vacant eyes, not knowing quite what had gone wrong. Then he felt the pain and began writhing, with his hand trying to plug the gaping hole in his gut.

Lee was in no mood for mercy. Kelly had lost his gun, but Lee wasn't about to give him a chance to find it again. With a calculated aim, Lee pulled the trigger of his Colt again and took off the top of Kelly's head. The man rolled, lifeless, onto the floor and Lee ran to Clemons' side. He was unconscious, but Lee could see that he had only a flesh wound, nothing a visit to the doctor and a few stitches couldn't take care of. While he was still bent over Clemons, Lee sensed another presence in the room. He immediately drew his gun, prepared to shoot the person who had just come through the back door.

It was Sue. Lee went to her, preventing her from seeing who was lying on the floor.

"Are you all right?" she asked, staring at the carnage all over her parlor.

"Of course," Lee replied hurriedly. "Now run and get the doctor. There's men hurt here and need attention."

Sue turned to do as Lee asked, but suddenly remembered why she had come in the first place. "Paxton," she said. "I hit him over the head in the jailhouse and ran over here. The deputy is still locked in the cell over there. If that man wakes up . . . oh goodness . . . Lee you'd better get over there right away. He helped me get out and you've got to help him."

* * *

Chook was lying flat on his belly with his arm stretched through the bars, trying his best to reach Paxton's gun. But Paxton was lying on the floor just inches out of reach—and rapidly regaining consciousness. Chook gave up, resigning himself to the fate that awaited him. Even if Paxton's men didn't get Morgan, Paxton would still get his revenge on Chook for double-crossing him and then get out of town before Morgan arrived. It was ironic, Chook thought as he sat back on the edge of the bunk. To be murdered in the very office he had sworn to uphold. There was nothing left to do but wait.

Chook relit the cigar Morgan had given him on the road in, savoring the last smoke he would ever have. Paxton was on his knees now, and shaking his head to clear his senses. An angry expression contorted his face. All at once he was on his feet, and all Chook could do was stand and watch, as helpless as a zoo animal.

Paxton looked around him, still dazed and wondering what had happened. Then he saw that the girl was gone. "Son-of-a-bitch!" he screamed. "You tricked me, you goddam bastard!" Paxton was insane with rage now. All he wanted to do was kill, and Chook was the only one handy.

"You and Morgan planned this whole thing. You let the girl out and now

Morgan's got her. All my plans. Everything I worked for—ruined!" Paxton picked up the gun laying on the floor and checked the load.

"Maybe Morgan will get away again this time, but at least I can have my revenge on you before I clear out." He leveled the gun on Chook and was amazed to see that the deputy was not begging for mercy.

"Not this time," Chook said. Then he took a deep drag on the cigar and tucked it into his jacket.

Lee and Sue were still standing in her living room when the whole house shook as if wracked by a thunderstorm. Sue looked puzzled but Lee knew exactly what the noise was. When the two finally made their way to the jailhouse, they found a huge crowd gathered and the entire side of the building blown away. There was no sign of either Chook or Paxton. Chook had remembered his dynamite.

Sue's face radiated joy, as much because she was finally alone with Lee as because she was safe. Despite Lee being anxious to get back and start repairs on the ranch, Sue had insisted on having Lee over for a home cooked supper—his first in months.

Lee was glad he had decided to stay. But he wasn't the only one having a good time. He had given both Luke and Sam twenty dollars in gold and staked them to a room in the Black Ace Saloon with a couple of Mary Spots' girls. There they could tell the story of their gunfight at Spade Bit until they were too drunk to repeat it. By morning, they would be as much heroes as Morgan or Chook.

Chook! It was a pity that he had lost his life after all, but Chook had expected it all along. But in the end he had forced himself to do what was right. Though it had cost him his own life, he had stood up to the most vicious outlaw Grover had ever seen—and won. And for that he could be proud to have called himself a lawman. Lee would have to see that his family back east received a long letter expounding on his deeds. Lee had been right. Chook hadn't been the coward he might have been.

"Lee," Sue said, snapping Lee out of his musings. "What on earth are you thinking about? Have you forgotten that I'm here?" She was offering him another glass of wine. Lee took a sip while she still held the goblet and flashed her a big smile.

"Oh—you!" she said. "You haven't changed a bit. Still your old playful self." She set both glasses down on the table beside the couch, then clasped her arms around his neck and looked deep into Lee's eyes. "You know," she said, "I really wondered whether you still cared enough to come. After all, you have been away for three months. Tell me, how do the women in Panama compare?''

"I came back, didn't I?'' Lee said slyly.

He slid closer to Sue and her arms tightened around him, pulling his lips toward her own. Lee knew his feelings for Sue had not changed. He was too deeply involved with her to even consider moving on and abandoning her forever. Their lips touched, furtively at first, then hungrily, as if trying to make up for all the months they had been apart.

Their lips separated and Sue buried her head in the warm, thick flesh of his neck. Her soft blonde hair brushed Lee's cheek, setting him on fire. He wanted her lips again, but when he pulled her away, he saw that her eyes were damp with tears.

"What is it?'' he asked. "Why are you crying?''

Sue didn't answer immediately. The words seemed stuck in her throat. "I— I'm just so happy to be back with you,'' she said at length. A little smile crept onto her lips again. She wiped the wetness from her eyes with a trembling hand, and Lee stroked her silky hair with his rough palm. She shivered and massaged the back of his neck, loosening the tense muscles.

Lee returned the smile but did not speak. Sue's skin was taut beneath the soft fabric of her clothes, and Lee sensed the anticipation she was experiencing. He began to move his hands over her, remembering every inch of her back, her shoulders, her arms. His hands finally slipped under her breasts, feeling the weight of them, wanting to know the touch of them against his own flesh.

He eagerly began unbuttoning her blouse, nervously fumbling with them as if for the first time, but pretending as though he was making her wait. As he worked his way down, he discovered that she had earlier removed all of her undergarments to make things easier and hasten their lovemaking. Her blouse parted in front and Sue arched toward him, pressing her breasts hard against the rough fabric of his shirt, letting the tips become red and erect. She pulled away from him, letting Lee get a good glimpse of the beautiful, white, red-tipped orbs.

They kissed deeply once again, then Sue asked, "Are you going to stay in those clothes all night?"

Lee stood, pulled off his jacket and began to unbutton his own shirt. Sue moved to her knees before him and began working on the lower half. She worked at his belt, and then at the buttons on his trousers, and finally pulled the pants down around Lee's knees. Though they had just eaten, she looked like a starved woman.

"What about my boots?" Lee said, laughing and sitting back on the couch. "First things first."

Sue looked embarrassed in her anxiousness, but quickly began tugging off his boots. Lee chipped in and soon both boots and pants were laying in a heap on the floor. Sue stood and stepped back. Lee stared as she reached back to unfasten her skirt, which made her ample breasts seem even more prominent. She smiled slowly as Lee admired her form.

She was only a few inches shorter than Lee, and her tall frame seemed exaggerated by her long, shapely legs, joining at the vortex by a hint of fine blood hair.

Sue began to tease him by caressing her own breasts, pinching the nipples to make them stand out for him. Lee stood and came to her and she immediately tucked her hand into the waistband of his underpants and tugged them to the floor. Lee kicked them off and pulled her to him, their naked bodies burning against each other.

He kissed her with tenderness. Then as if bowing before some unknown icon, Lee bent and kissed one breast, letting his tongue linger over the fruitlike tip. She sighed deeply, then shuddered, sending a wave of gooseflesh over her body.

She fell against him and he slid a strong

arm around her waist, lifting her and carrying her, then placing her gently on the couch. The heat from the fireplace and from their own passion coated their bodies with perspiration and made them burn with anticipation.

"Oh, Lee," she said, looking up at him from the couch. "Please just stand there a moment and let me look at you. It's been so long."

Lee did as she asked, standing still in the orange glow of the fire, so she could savor every ripple of muscle, every sculpted angle of his bare flesh. His tanned body glistened with sweat, and every hair felt as if it were standing on end.

Sue's gaze began with his eyes, which radiated a brilliant blue against the ochre glow in the room. But her eyes quickly fell to his huge chest and arms, the same that had held her so close moments before. Finally there was the beautiful organ hanging in wait between his powerful legs.

Her hand reached out and touched his calf, kneading his flesh, then traced a path up his thigh until she reached the object of her desire. She cupped her hand under his balls, · squeezing them gently until Lee's eyes rolled back in his head and he began to moan in pleasure. Blood was rushing into his cock, and it slowly inched its way to stiffness. Sue ran her delicate fingers along the hardening shaft, then gripped it in her fist, increasing the pressure until the tip of it mushroomed out and turned a brilliant red.

Lee placed his hands on his hips and began to pump them backward and forward until Sue picked up the rhythm with her hand. When he was fully erect, Sue leaned toward him and touched the tip of her tongue to the head, letting the drop of semen that had formed, stretch out into a long clear strand. When it broke, she licked her lips to taste him, then parted her mouth to let the entire shaft inside.

Once his entire organ was coated with saliva, she returned her hand and began pumping in earnest, sliding her hand over his foreskin with such dexterity that Lee thought he would burst. Sue knew she was getting him excited and she began to jerk him even faster. She wanted to watch him come, to shoot his load right there in front of her face. She had never seen a man come before. Not like that. Every man she had had before Lee had been on and off her in a matter of minutes. Only Lee had taken the time to really make love to her. Now she was about to watch her lover do what he had done inside her many times before. She would stroke him until his magic fluid shot out of him.

But Lee was not ready just yet. He wanted to savor their evening of lovemaking as long as he could, to enjoy much longer the pleasure she was giving him, and give her a reunion to remember as well. Lee gently removed her protesting hand. "Not just yet," he said. "We have all night for that."

Lee bent and kissed her pouting lips. Then he fell to his knees, forgetting his own pleasure and concentrating on her own. He nibbled her neck, her heaving breasts, her flat stomach, slowly working his way down to the musky scent that was unique to this woman. He placed a hand on one of her knees and urged her legs apart. He kissed his way down her thigh to the wetness that had soaked the few strands of blonde hair that curled between her legs.

With his fingers he pushed them aside to reveal the swollen pink lips, slightly parted as if inviting him to enter into the depths beyond. Without any encouragement, Sue lifted her hips toward his open mouth, and Lee slid his tongue easily inside her. Sue let out a little gasp and thrust her buttocks higher as if she were trying to fill herelf with a tiny cock. Lee darted his tongue rapidly and made her squeal, then he pursed his lips and sucked on the little button nestled within the folds of flesh.

"Oh, God, Lee. It feels so good. You couldn't know how good," she said, gasping for air. "I want you to fill me with that thing of yours." Sue pulled his head up from between her legs. Lee wiped his dripping mouth and moved over her, as Sue threw one of her legs over the back of the sofa to give him greater access to her. Lee wasted no time, but plunged his organ full length into her.

This was too much for Sue to bear. The sensation of his rod thrusting into her sent her into wave after wave of orgasm. So intense was it that she clawed at Lee's back as if to grasp onto something that would keep her from falling into oblivion. She pumped her hips and trembled under Lee Morgan's weight, begging for more, yet pleading for the uncontrollable spasms to end.

Lee was on the brink as well, nearly unable to contain himself. His cock throbbed in her viselike grip, and his balls constricted as if gathering strength for the inevitable explosion. Sue finally relaxed under him, allowing him to stroke as quickly or as slowly as he wanted.

All at once he came out of her and Sue understood just what he meant for her to do. She had wanted to see him come and now he was obliging her desire. He sat on his knees above her and Sue grasped him toward the base of his organ, immediately continuing the steady rhythm. She stared at his ripening head and watched as it swelled to even greater dimensions.

He came with a force that even she hadn't expected. The first jet of white liquid shot onto her neck and breasts. She couldn't take her eyes off of him as he spurt again and again, sending streams of hot spunk onto her belly and running down her fingers. Lee collapsed onto her, exhausted, smothering her with grateful kisses, and whispering his love for her.

The next morning over breakfast, neither spoke a word about the passion of the evening before, though Lee noticed that Sue was almost glowing with joy.

"So, what will you do now?" she asked Lee. "Do you think you might stick around a while this time, or do you plan to go off and conquer all of South America?" Her words were not mean-spirited, and Lee knew immediately what she was leading up to.

"First thing I have to do is hire some good men and get Spade Bit back into shape," he replied. "It's seen a lot of neglect this summer. The stock is in bad shape . . ."

"And what of us?" Sue cut in, getting right to the point.

Lee looked at her, sorry that he was unable to give her the answer she wanted just yet. "You know I love you dearly, Sue," he said. "But right now there are too many things I have to take care of before I can even consider marriage again. Besides, there's plenty more men like Paxton out there that could do me a lot of harm through you. Surely you understand that."

Sue didn't respond. She would let him off the hook until he had resettled. He couldn't keep giving her excuses forever. One day, in his own time, Lee would ask her. She didn't mind the wait. A man like Lee Morgan never rushed into anything that didn't involve gunplay.

With Paxton safely sleeping in potters field, Grover quickly returned to normal. The townspeople all chipped in to give Chook a hero's funeral, and everyone within an hour of the place came to see him buried.

Among the guests was Marshal Rayburn, who had come all the way from Boise for the occasion. Dressed in his finest uniform, he had first ridden out to Spade Bit to personally thank Lee Morgan for setting things straight in Grover.

As they sat in Lee's parlor discussing the events over a cup of coffee, Lee couldn't help but notice that Rayburn could not sit still, as if there was something on his mind that he was having trouble bringing up. "Something eating at you, Marshal?" Lee finally said to break the ice. "You look a mite nervous."

Rayburn sat back in his chair, glad that Morgan had prompted him. It would make what he had to say that much easier. "As a matter of fact, there is," he said. "You and I both know that despite all the hoopla in town over Chook blowing Paxton to kingdom come, Chook wasn't much of a lawman. In fact he was the most pitiful excuse for a deputy I've ever hired."

"I won't argue with that," Lee said.

"Frankly, I only gave him the job because no one else in town wanted it at the time. Ain't too many men willing to risk their necks to keep the peace in these parts. But times have changed since then. Grover's nearly doubled in size, and I don't aim to put another incompetent in Chook's seat. Lee, I came out here as much to talk to you as attend this funeral. Despite your reputation as a gunman, word's reached me even in Boise that you're just about the most honest man in these parts."

Rayburn reached into his shirt pocket, pulled out a shiny tin star and tossed it into Lee's lap. "That's why I believe you would do the town a great service to put that on your lapel beginning today. The pay ain't much, but with your name on the jailhouse door, you'd be doing a lot to keep the peace for miles around. I need a man I can count on. What do you say, Morgan?"

Lee picked up the star and looked into his reflection. He didn't have to make the marshal wait for an answer. "I'm mighty honored," he said. "And a few years ago I might have taken you up on the offer. But right now, I have a ranch that I'm determined to take care of. 'Sides, I'm not eager to be looking over my shoulder every time I walk down the street. I've made a lot of enemies in my day, and once they get wind that I'm the new Sheriff of Grover, there's apt to be folks comin' out of the woodwork to get back at me."

The marshal sighed and took a sip of coffee. "Well, I thought it might be worth a chance, comin' out to see what your feelings were on the matter. Never any harm in asking."

Lee looked at the star again and, to Rayburn's amazement, tucked it into his shirt pocket. "I just got an idea," Lee said. "Will you excuse me a moment?"

"Sure," Rayburn said, wondering what Lee was up to. "Funeral ain't till this afternoon."

Lee stood up and went out the front door to the barn. A few moments later he returned with Sam Lawton in tow. When Sam saw the marshal, he was very confused. "What's going on here, Mr. Morgan? Have I done something wrong?"

Rayburn looked over the tall young man

standing before him, suddenly knowing what was on Morgan's mind. Without Morgan saying a word, Rayburn nodded his head in assent. "Who might this be?" Rayburn asked.

"This here's Sam Lawton," he said. "I think he might be willin' to listen to your offer."

"What offer?" Sam said, trying to figure out what these two crazy men were talking and smiling about. "What are you two talking about? Why have you got me in here? I've got a lot of work to do."

Lee pulled out the star and without warning, pinned it onto Sam's jacket pocket. Sam's eyes popped open when he saw it. "The marshal here thinks you'd make a fine sheriff, and stopped by to see if I could spare you," Lee lied. "I told him you were the best man I had but he's about convinced me that the town needs a good lawman more. What do you say, Sam? I'm leaving it up to you."

"I don't know what to say," Sam said. "I ain't never really thought about nothing like this before. All I know is horses."

"And next time I come down here you'll know all about sheriffing," the marshal said, not willing to take no for an answer twice in one day.

"You'd better get your gear together," Lee instructed. "Everyone's goin' in for

Chook's funeral this afternoon, and there ain't no better time for a swearing-in ceremony. You'll ride in with us in an hour. And don't you take that badge off, either."

"I'm packin' right now," Sam said. He pushed his hat back onto his head and rushed out of the room and back to the barn.

Lee and Rayburn both shared a hearty laugh at the man's consternation. Then the marshal added on a more serious note: "Lee, do you think he can handle it? After all, he ain't much more than a boy."

"You got anyone better in mind?" Lee asked, still laughing. "Don't you worry none, Marshal. He'll do just fine. He'll be a real professional by the time you get down this way again. Everyone in town knows he's a good man. He'll have all the respect he needs. And if there's any trouble, I'll make sure he knows he can turn to me for help. But there ain't apt to be much. All Grover needs is an honest man to set a good example. And Sam's about the finest example you'll find anywhere."

"I appreciate that, Lee," the marshal said, watching Lee go to the front window and part the curtains. "I'm inclined to take your word for it."

But Lee Morgan didn't hear the marshal's thanks. He was too busy watching the young man standing by the barn door showing off his new badge, the symbol of respectability that he had earned over the last two days.

Lee saw in him everything Frank Leslie had wanted him to be when he became a man, everything that Lee Morgan had rejected in order to earn respectability the hard way—with the barrel of a gun.